Henrik Ibsen, F. Anstey

The Pocket Ibsen

A collection of some of the master's best-known dramas

Henrik Ibsen, F. Anstey

The Pocket Ibsen
A collection of some of the master's best-known dramas

ISBN/EAN: 9783337219932

Printed in Europe, USA, Canada, Australia, Japan

Cover: Foto ©Andreas Hilbeck / pixelio.de

More available books at **www.hansebooks.com**

THE
POCKET IBSEN

*A COLLECTION OF SOME OF THE MASTER'S
BEST-KNOWN DRAMAS*

CONDENSED, REVISED, AND SLIGHTLY
RE-ARRANGED FOR THE BENEFIT OF THE
EARNEST STUDENT

BY

F. ANSTEY

AUTHOR OF "VICE VERSA," "VOCES POPULI," ETC.

WITH

ILLUSTRATIONS BY BERNARD PARTRIDGE

NEW AND ENLARGED EDITION

LONDON
WILLIAM HEINEMANN
1895

FIRST EDITION, *May 1893*

ERRATA

For "Rosmershölm" *read* "Rosmersholm"

P. 143, l. 9, *for* "My father's sight failing !" *read* "Old Werle's sight failing !"

PREFATORY NOTE

"*PILL-DOCTOR HERDAL*" *is, as the observant reader will instantly perceive, rather a reverent attempt to tread in the footprints of the Norwegian dramatist, than a version of any actually existing masterpiece. The author is conscious that his imitation is painfully lacking in the mysterious obscurity of the original, that the vein of allegorical symbolism is thinner throughout than it should be, and that the characters are not nearly so mad as persons invariably are in real life—but these are the faults inevitable to a 'prentice hand, and he trusts that due allowances may be made for them by the critical.*

In conclusion he wishes to express his acknowledgments to Messrs. Bradbury and Agnew for their permission to reprint the present volume, the contents of which made their original appearance in the pages of " Punch."

CONTENTS

ROSMERSHÖLM

A

ROSMERSHÖLM

ACT FIRST

Sitting-room at Rosmersholm, with a stove, flower-stand, windows, ancient and modern ancestors, doors, and everything handsome about it. REBECCA WEST *is sitting knitting a large antimacassar which is nearly finished. Now and then she looks out of a window, and smiles and nods expectantly to someone outside.* MADAM HELSETH *is laying the table for supper.*

REBECCA.

[*Folding up her work slowly.*] But tell me precisely, what about this white horse?   [*Smiling quietly.*

Madam Helseth.

Lord forgive you, Miss !—[*fetching cruet-stand, and placing it on table*]—but you're making fun of me !

Rebecca.

[*Gravely.*] No, indeed. Nobody makes fun at Rosmersholm. Mr. Rosmer would not understand it. [*Shutting window.*] Ah, here is Rector Kroll. [*Opening door.*] You will stay to supper, will you not, Rector, and I will tell them to give us some little extra dish.

Kroll.

[*Hanging up his hat in the hall.*] Many thanks. [*Wipes his boots.*] May I come in ? [*Comes in, puts down his stick, sits down, and looks about him.*] And how do you and Rosmer get on together, eh ?

Rebecca.

Ever since your sister, Beata, went mad and jumped into the mill-race, we have been as happy as two little birds together. [*After a pause, sitting down in arm-chair.*] So you don t really mind my living here all alone with Rosmer? We were afraid you might, perhaps.

KROLL.

Why, how on earth—on the contrary, I shouldn't object at all if you—[*looks at her meaningly*]—h'm !

REBECCA.

[*Interrupting, gravely.*] For shame, Rector; how can you make such jokes ?

KROLL.

[*As if surprised.*] Jokes ! We do not joke in these parts—but here is Rosmer.

> [*Enter* ROSMER, *gently and softly.*

ROSMER.

So, my dear old friend, you have come again, after a year's absence. [*Sits down.*] We almost thought that——

KROLL.

[*Nods.*] So Miss West was saying—but you are quite mistaken. I merely thought I might remind you, if I came, of our poor Beata's suicide, so I kept away. We Norwegians are not without our simple tact.

ROSMER.

It was considerate—but unnecessary. Reb — I *mean*, Miss West—and I often allude to the incident, do we not?

REBECCA.

[*Strikes Tändstickor.*] Oh yes, indeed. [*Lighting lamp.*] Whenever we feel a little more cheerful than usual.

KROLL.

You dear good people! [*Wanders up the room.*] I came because the Spirit of Revolt has crept into my School. A Secret Society has existed for weeks in the Lower Third! To-day it has come to my knowledge that a booby trap was prepared for me by the

hand of my own son, Laurits, and I then discovered
that a hair had been inserted in my cane by my
daughter Hilda! The only way in which a right-
minded Schoolmaster can combat this anarchic and
subversive spirit is to start a newspaper, and I
thought that you, as a weak, credulous, inexperienced
and impressionable kind of man, were the very person
to be the Editor.

[REBECCA *laughs softly, as if to herself.*
ROSMER *jumps up and sits down again.*

REBECCA.

[*With a look at Rosmer.*] Tell him now!

ROSMER.

[*Returning the look.*] I can't—Some other evening.
Well, perhaps—— [*To* KROLL.] I can't be your
Editor—because [*in a low voice*] I—I am on
the side of Laurits and Hilda!

KROLL.

[*Looks from one to the other, gloomily.*] H'm!

ROSMER.

Yes. Since we last met, I have changed my views.
I am going to create a new democracy, and awaken it
to its true task of making all the people of this
country noblemen, by freeing their wills, and
purifying their minds !

KROLL.

What *do* you mean !   [*Takes up his hat.*

ROSMER.

[*Bowing his head.*] I don't quite know, my dear
friend; it was Reb—— I should say Miss West's
scheme.

KROLL.

H'm ! [*A suspicion appears in his face.*] Now I
begin to believe that what Beata said about schemes
——no matter. But under the circumstances, I will
not stay to supper.

[*Takes up his stick, and walks out.*

ROSMER.

I *told* you he would be annoyed. I shall go to bed now. I don't want any supper. [*He lights a candle, and goes out; presently his footsteps are heard over-head, as he undresses.* REBECCA *pulls a bell-rope.*

REBECCA.

[*To* MADAM HELSETH, *who enters with dishes.*] No, Mr. Rosmer will not have supper to-night. [*In a lighter tone.*] Perhaps he is afraid of the nightmare. There are so many sorts of White Horses in this world!

MADAM HELSETH.

[*Shaking.*] Lord! lord! that Miss West—the things she does say!

[REBECCA *goes out through door, knitting antimacassar thoughtfully, as Curtain falls.*

ACT SECOND

ROSMER'S *study. Doors and windows, bookshelves, a writing-table. Door, with curtain, leading to* ROSMER'S *bedroom.* ROSMER *discovered in a smoking jacket cutting a pamphlet with a paper-knife. There is a knock at the door.* ROSMER *says "Come in."* REBECCA *enters in a morning wrapper and curl-papers. She sits on a chair close to* ROSMER, *and looks over his shoulder as he cuts the leaves.* RECTOR KROLL *is shown up.*

KROLL.

[*Lays his hat on the table and looks at* REBECCA *from head to foot.*] I am really afraid that I am in the way.

REBECCA.

[*Surprised.*] Because I am in my morning wrapper and curl-papers? You forget that I am *emancipated*, Rector Kroll.

[*She leaves them and listens behind curtain in* ROSMER'S *bedroom.*

ROSMER.

Yes, Miss West and I have worked our way forward in faithful comradeship.

KROLL.

[*Shakes his head at him slowly.*] So I perceive. Miss West is naturally inclined to be forward. But, I say, *really* you know—— However, I came to tell you that poor Beata was not so mad as she looked, though flowers *did* bewilder her so. [*Taking off his gloves meaningly.*] She jumped into the mill-race because she had an idea that you ought to marry Miss West !

Rosmer.

[*Jumps half up from his chair.*] I? Marry—Miss West! My good gracious, Kroll! I don't *under-stand*, it is *most* incomprehensible. [*Looks fixedly before him.*] How can people?—— [*Looks at him for a moment, then rises.*] Will you get out? [*Still quiet and self-restrained.*] But first tell me why you never mentioned this before?

Kroll.

Why? Because I thought you were both orthodox, which made all the difference. Now I know that you side with Laurits and Hilda, and mean to make the democracy into noblemen, and accordingly I intend to make it hot for you in my paper. *Good morning!*

> [*He slams the door with spite as* Rebecca *enters from bed-room.*

Rosmer.

[*As if surprised.*] You—in my bedroom! You have been listening, dear? But you *are* so emancipated.

"Taking off his gloves meaningly"

Ah, well! so our pure and beautiful friendship has been misinterpreted, bespattered! Just because you wear a morning wrapper, and have lived here alone for a year, people with coarse souls and ignoble eyes make unpleasant remarks! But what really *did* drive Beata mad? *Why* did she jump into the mill-race? I'm sure we did everything we could to spare her! I made it the business of my life to keep her in ignorance of all our interests—*didn't* I, now?

REBECCA.

You did. But why brood over it? What *does* it matter? Get on with your great beautiful task, dear —[*approaching him cautiously from behind*]—winning over minds and wills, and creating noblemen, you know—*joyful* noblemen!

ROSMER.

[*Walking about restlessly, as if in thought.*] Yes, I know. I have never laughed in the whole course of my life—we Rosmers don't—and so I felt that

spreading gladness and light, and making the democracy joyful, was properly my mission. But *now*—I
feel too upset to go on, Rebecca, unless—— [*Shakes
his head heavily.*] Yes, an idea has just occurred to
me—— [*Looks at her, and then runs his hands through
his hair*]—Oh, my goodness! No—I *can't*.

[*He leans his elbows on table.*

REBECCA.

Be a free man to the full, Rosmer—tell me your
idea.

ROSMER.

[*Gloomily.*] I don't know what you'll say to it.
It's this: Our platonic comradeship was all very
well while I was peaceful and happy. Now that I
am bothered and badgered, I feel—*why*, I can't
exactly explain, but I *do* feel that I must oppose a
new and living reality to the gnawing memories of
the past. I should perhaps, explain that this is
equivalent to an Ibsenian proposal.

Rebecca.

[*Catches at the chairback with joy.*] How? at *last*—
a rise at last! [*Recollects herself.*] But what am I
about? Am I not an emancipated enigma? [*Puts
her hands over her ears as if in terror.*] What are
you saying? You mustn't. I can't *think* what you
mean. Go away, do!

Rosmer.

[*Softly.*] Be the new and living reality. It is
the only way to put Beata out of the Saga. Shall
we try it?

Rebecca.

Never! Do not—*do* not ask me why—for I haven't
a notion—but never! [*Nods slowly to him and rises.*]
White Horses would not induce me! [*With her hand
on door-handle.*] Now you *know*! [*She goes out!*

Rosmer.

[*Sits up, stares, thunderstruck, at the stove, and says
to himself.*] Well—I—am——

Quick Curtain.

ACT THIRD

*Sitting-room at Rosmersholm. Sun shining outside
in the Garden. Inside* REBECCA WEST *is water-
ing a geranium with a small watering-pot.
Her crochet antimacassar lies in the arm-chair.*
MADAME HELSETH *is rubbing the chairs with
furniture-polish from a large bottle. Enter*
ROSMER, *with his hat and stick in his hand.*
MADAME HELSETH *corks the bottle and goes out
to the right.*

REBECCA.

Good morning, dear. [*A moment after—crocheting.*]
Have you seen Rector Kroll's paper this morning?
There's something about *you* in it

ROSMER.

Oh, indeed? [*Puts down hat and stick, and takes*

up paper]. H'm! [*Reads—then walks about the room.*] Kroll *has* made it hot for me. [*Reads some more.*] Oh, this is *too* bad! Rebecca, they *do* say such nasty spiteful things! they actually call me a renegade— and I can't *think* why! They *mustn't* go on like this. All that is good in human nature will go to ruin if they're allowed to attack an excellent man like me! Only think, if I can make them see how unkind they have been!

REBECCA.

Yes, dear, in that you have a great and glorious object to attain—and I wish you may get it!

ROSMER.

Thanks. I think I shall. [*Happens to look through window and jumps.*] Ah, no, I shan't—never now, I have just seen——

REBECCA.

Not the White Horse, dear? We must really not overdo that White Horse!

ROSMER.

No —the mill-race, where Beata——[*Puts on his hat -takes it off again.*] I'm beginning to be haunted by —no, I *don't* mean the Horse —by a terrible suspicion that Beata may have been right after all! Yes, I do believe, now I come to think of it, that I must really have been in love with you from the first. Tell me *your* opinion.

REBECCA.

[*Struggling with herself, and still crocheting.*] Oh —I can't exactly say—such an odd question to ask me!

ROSMER.

[*Shakes his head.*] Perhaps; I have no sense of humour—no respectable Norwegian *has*- and I *do* want to know—because, you see, if I *was* in love with you, it was a *sin*, and if I once convinced myself of that——

[*Wanders across the room.*

REBECCA

[*Breaking out.*] Oh, these old ancestral prejudices! Here is your hat, and your stick, too; go and take a walk.

> [ROSMER *takes hat and stick, first, then goes out and takes a walk: presently* MADAM HELSETH *appears, and tells* REBECCA *something.* REBECCA *tells her something. They whisper together.* MADAM HELSETH *nods, and shows in* RECTOR KROLL, *who keeps his hat in his hand, and sits on a chair.*

KROLL.

I merely called for the purpose of informing you that I consider you an artful and designing person, but that, on the whole, considering your birth and moral antecedents, you know—[*nods at her*]—it is not surprising. [REBECCA *walks about wringing her hands.*] Why, what *is* the matter? Did you really not know that you had no right to your father's name? I'd no *idea* you would mind my mentioning such a trifle!

REBECCA.

[*Breaking out.*] I *do* mind. I am an emancipated enigma, but I retain a few little prejudices still. I *don't* like owning to my real age, and I *do* prefer to be legitimate. And, after your information—of which I was quite ignorant, as my mother, the late Mrs. Gamvik, never *once* alluded to it—I feel I must confess everything. Strong-minded advanced women are like that. Here is Rosmer. [ROSMER *enters with his hat and stick.*] Rosmer, I want to tell you and Rector Kroll a little story. Let us sit down, dear, all three of us. [*They sit down, mechanically, on chairs.*] A long time ago, before the play began—[*in a voice scarcely audible*]—in Ibsenite dramas, all the interesting things somehow *do* happen before the play begins——

Rosmer.

But, Rebecca, I *know* all this.

Kroll.

[*Looks hard at her.*] Perhaps I had better go?

Rebecca.

No—I will be short· This was it. I wanted to take my share in the life of the New Era, and march onward with Rosmer. There was one dismal, insurmountable barrier—[*to* Rosmer, *who nods gravely*]—Beata! I understood where your deliverance lay—and I acted. *I* drove Beata into the mill-race. . . . There!

Rosmer.

[*After a short silence*]. H'm! Well, Kroll—[*takes up his hat*]—if you're thinking of walking home, I'll go too. I'm going to be orthodox once more—after *this!*

Kroll.

[*Severely and impressively, to* Rebecca.] A nice sort of young woman *you* are! [*Both go out hastily, without looking at* Rebecca.

Rebecca.

[*Speaks to herself, under her breath.*] Now I have done it. I wonder *why*. [*Pulls bell-rope.*] Madam Helseth, I have just had a glimpse of two rushing White Horses. Bring down my hair-trunk.

> [*Enter* Madam Helseth, *with large hair-trunk, as Curtain falls.*

ACT FOUR

Late evening. REBECCA WEST *stands by a lighted lamp,*
with a shade over it, packing sandwiches, &c., in a
reticule, with a faint smile. The antimacassar is
on the sofa. Enter ROSMER.

ROSMER.

[*Seeing the sandwiches, &c.*] Sandwiches? Then
you are going! Why, on earth—I *can't* understand!

REBECCA.

Dear, you never *can.* Rosmersholm is too much
for me. But how did you get on with Kroll?

ROSMER.

We have made it up. He has convinced me that
the work of ennobling men was several sizes too large
for me—so I am going to let it alone——

REBECCA.

[*With her faint smile.*] There I almost think, dear, that you are wise.

ROSMER.

[*As if annoyed.*] What, so *you* don't believe in me either, Rebecca—you never *did!*

[*Sits listlessly on chair.*

REBECCA.

Not much, dear, when you are left to yourself— but I've another confession to make

ROSMER.

What, *another?* I really can't stand any more confessions just now!

REBECCA.

[*Sitting close to him.*] It is only a little one. I bullied Beata into the mill-race—because of a wild uncontrollable—— [ROSMER *mores uneasily.*] Sit still, dear—uncontrollable fancy—for *you!*

Rosmer.

[*Goes and sits on sofa.*] Oh, my goodness, Rebecca —you *mustn't*, you know ! .

> [*He jumps up and down as if embarrassed.*

Rebecca.

Don't be alarmed, dear, it is all over now. After living alone with you in solitude, when you showed me all your thoughts without reserve—little by little, somehow the fancy passed off. I caught the Rosmer view of life badly, and dulness descended on my soul as an extinguisher upon one of our Northern dips. The Rosmer view of life is ennobling, very—but hardly lively. And I've more yet to tell you.

Rosmer.

[*Turning it off.*] Isn't that enough for one evening ?

Rebecca.

[*Almost voiceless.*] No, dear. I have a Past—*behind* me !

ROSMER.

Behind you? How strange. I had an idea of that sort already. [*Starts, as if in fear.*] A joke! [*Sadly.*] Ah, no—*no*, I must not give way to *that!* Never mind the Past, Rebecca; I once thought that I had made the grand discovery that, if one is only virtuous, one will be happy. I see now it was too daring, too original—an immature dream. What bothers me is that I can't—somehow I *can't* believe entirely in you—I am not even sure that I *have* ennobled you so very much—*isn't* it terrible?

REBECCA.

[*Wringing her hands.*] Oh, this killing doubt! [*Looks darkly at him.*] Is there anything *I* can do to convince you?

ROSMER.

[*As if impelled to speak against his will.*] Yes, one thing—only I'm afraid you wouldn't see it in the same light. And yet I must mention it. It is like this.

" Oh, my goodness, Rebecca—you *mustn't*, you know ! "

I want to recover faith in my mission, in my power
to ennoble human souls. And, as a logical thinker,
this I cannot do now, unless—well, unless you jump
into the mill-race, too, like Beata !

REBECCA.

[*Takes up her antimacassar, with composure, and
puts it on her head.*] Anything to oblige you.

ROSMER.

[*Springs up.*] What? You really *will!* You are
sure you don't mind? Then, Rebecca, I will go
further. I will even go—yes—as far as you go
yourself !

REBECCA.

[*Bows her head towards his breast.*] You will see me
off? Thanks. Now you are indeed an Ibsenite.

[*Smiles almost imperceptibly.*

ROSMER.

[*Cautiously.*] I said as far as *you* go. I don't
commit myself further than that. Shall we go ?

REBECCA.

First tell me this. Are *you* going with *me*, or am *I* going with *you*?

ROSMER.

A subtle psychological point—but we have not time to think it out here. We will discuss it as we go along. Come!

[ROSMER *takes his hat and stick,* REBECCA *her reticule, with sandwiches. They go out hand-in-hand through the door, which they leave open. The room (as is not uncommon with rooms in Norway) is left empty. Then* MADAM HELSETH *enters through another door.*

MADAM HELSETH.

The cab, Miss—not here! [*Looks out.*] Out to-gether—at this time of night—upon my—*not* on the garden seat? [*Looks out of window.*] My goodness! *what* is that white thing on the bridge—the *Horse* at last! [*Shrieks aloud.*] And those two sinful creatures running home!

Enter ROSMER *and* REBECCA, *out of breath.*

ROSMER.

[*Scarcely able to get the words out.*] It's no use, Rebecca—we must put it off till another evening. We can't be expected to jump off a footbridge which already has a White Horse on it. And if it comes to that, why should we jump at all? I know now that I really *have* ennobled you, which was all *I* wanted. What would be the good of recovering faith in my mission at the bottom of a mill-pond? No, Rebecca—[*Lays his hand on her head*]—there is no judge over us, and therefore——

REBECCA.

[*Interrupting gravely.*] We will bind ourselves over in our own recognisances to come up for judgment when called upon.

> [MADAM HELSETH *holds on to a chair-back.*
> REBECCA *finishes the antimacassar calmly as Curtain falls.*

NORA; OR, THE BIRD-CAGE

(ET DIKKISVÖET)

NORA: OR, THE BIRD-CAGE
(ET DIKKISVÖET)

ACT FIRST

A room tastefully filled with cheap Art-furniture.
Gimcracks in an étagère: a festoon of chenille
monkeys hanging from the gaselier. Japanese
fans, skeletons, cotton-wool spiders, frogs and
lizards, scattered everywhere about. Drain-pipes
with tall dyed grasses. A porcelain stove decorated
with transferable pictures. Showily-bound books
in book-case. Window. The Visitor's bell rings
in the hall outside. The hall-door is heard to
open, and then to shut. Presently NORA *walks in*
with parcels; a porter carries a large Christmas-

tree after her—which he puts down. NORA gives
him a shilling—and he goes out grumbling.
NORA *hums contentedly, and eats macaroons. Then*
HELMER *puts his head out of his Manager's room,*
and NORA *hides macaroons cautiously.*

HELMER.

[*Playfully.*] Is that my little squirrel twittering—
that my lark frisking in here?

NORA.

Ess! [*To herself.*] I have only been married eight
years, so these marital amenities have not yet had
time to pall!

HELMER.

[*Threatening with his finger.*] I hope the little bird
has surely not been digging its beak into any
macaroons, eh?

NORA.

[*Bolting one, and wiping her mouth.*] No, most
certainly not. [*To herself.*] The worst of being so

babyish is—one *does* have to tell such a lot of tara-
diddles! [*To* HELMER.] See what *I've* bought—it's
been *such* fun!   [*Hums.*

HELMER.

[*Inspecting parcels.*] H'm—rather an *expensive*
little lark !   [*Takes her playfully by the ear.*

NORA.

Little birds like to have a flutter occasionally.
Which reminds me—— [*Plays with his coat-buttons.*]
I'm such a simple ickle sing—but if you *are* thinking
of giving me a Christmas present, make it cash !

HELMER.

Just like your poor father, *he* always asked me to
make it cash—he never made any himself! It's
heredity, I suppose. Well—well !

[*Goes back to his Bank.* NORA *goes on humming.*

Enter Mrs. Linden, *doubtfully.*

Nora.

What, Christina—why, how old you look! But then you are poor. I'm not. Torvald has just been made a Bank Manager. [*Tidies the room.*] Isn't it really wonderfully delicious to be well off? But of course, you wouldn't know. *We* were poor once, and, do you know, when Torvald was ill, I—[*tossing her head*]—though I *am* such a frivolous little squirrel, and all that, I actually borrowed £300 for him to go abroad. Wasn't *that* clever? Tra-la-la! I shan't tell you *who* lent it. I didn't even tell Torvald. I am such a mere baby I don't tell him everything. I tell Dr. Rank, though. Oh, I'm so awfully happy I should like to shout, " Dash it all!"

Mrs. Linden.

[*Stroking her hair.*] Do—it is a natural and innocent outburst—you are such a child! But I am a widow, and want employment. *Do* you think your husband could find me a place as clerk in his Bank ? [*Proudly.*] I am an excellent knitter!

Nora.

That would really be awfully funny. [*To* Helmer, *who enters.*] Torvald, this is Christina ; she wants to be a clerk in your Bank—*do* let her! She thinks such a lot of *you*. [*To herself.*] Another taradiddle !

Helmer.

She is a sensible woman, and deserves encouragement. Come along, Mrs. Linden, and we'll see what we can do for you.

> [*He goes out through the hall with* Mrs.
> Linden, *and the front-door is heard to
> slam after them.*

Nora.

[*Opens door, and calls.*] Now, Emmy, Ivar, and Bob, come in and have a romp with Mamma—we will play hide-and-seek. [*She gets under the table, smiling in quiet satisfaction;* KROGSTAD *enters—*NORA *pounces out upon him.*] Boo! . . . Oh, I *beg* your pardon. I don't do this kind of thing *generally—* though I may be a little silly.

KROGSTAD.

[*Politely.*] Don't mention it. I called because I happened to see your husband go out with Mrs. Linden—from which, being a person of considerable penetration, I infer that he is about to give her my post at the Bank. Now, as you owe me the balance of £300, for which I hold your acknowledgment, you will see the propriety of putting a stop to this little game at once.

NORA.

But I don't at all—not a little wee bit! I'm so childish, you know—why *should* I ?

[*Sitting upright on carpet.*

KROGSTAD.

I will try to make it plain to the meanest capacity. When you came to me for the loan, I naturally

"Boo!"

required some additional security. Your father, being
a shady Government official, without a penny—for, if
he had possessed one, he would presumably have left
it to you—without a penny. then—I, as a cautious
man of business, insisted upon having his signature
as a surety. Oh, we Norwegians are sharp fellows !

Nora.

Well, you *got* papa's signature, didn't you ?

Krogstad.

Oh, I *got* it right enough.   Unfortunately, it was
dated three days after his decease—now, how do you
account for *that ?*

Nora.

How ?   Why, as poor Papa was dead, and couldn't
sign. I signed *for* him, that's all !   Only somehow I
forgot to put the date back.   *That's* how.   Didn't I
tell you I was a silly, unbusiness like little thing ?
It's very simple.

KROGSTAD.

Very—but what you did amounts to forgery, notwithstanding. I happen to know, because I'm a lawyer, and have done a little in the forging way myself. So, to come to the point—if *I* get kicked out, I shall not go alone !   [*He bows, and goes out.*

NORA.

It *can't* be wrong ! Why, no one but Krogstad would have been taken in by it ! If the Law says it's wrong, the Law's a goose—a bigger goose than poor little me even ! [*To* HELMER, *who enters.*] Oh, Torvald, how you made me jump !

HELMER.

Has anybody called ? [NORA *shakes her head.*] Oh, my little squirrel mustn't tell naughty whoppers Why, I just met that fellow Krogstad in the hall. He's been asking you to get me to take him back—now, hasn't he ?

Nora.

[*Walking about.*] Do just see how pretty the Christmas-tree looks!

Helmer.

Never mind the tree—I want to have this out about Krogstad. I can't take him back, because many years ago he forged a name. As a lawyer, a close observer of human nature, and a Bank Manager, I have remarked that people who forge names seldom or never confide the fact to their children—which inevitably brings moral contagion into the entire family. From which it follows, logically, that Krogstad has been poisoning his children for years by acting a part, and is morally lost. [*Stretches out his hands to her.*] I can't bear a morally lost Bank-cashier about me!

Nora.

But you never thought of dismissing him till Christina came!

HELMER.

H'm! I've got some business to attend to —so
good-bye, little lark! [*Goes into office and shuts door.*

NORA.

[*Pale with terror.*] If Krogstad poisons his children
because he once forged a name, I must be poisoning
Emmy, and Bob, and Ivar, because *I* forged papa's
signature! [*Short pause ; she raises her head proudly.*]
After all, if I *am* a doll, I can still draw a logical
inference! I mustn't play with the children any
more—[*hotly*]—I don't care—I *shall*, though! Who
cares for Krogstad?

> [*She makes a face, choking with suppressed
> tears, as Curtain falls.*

ACT SECOND

*The room, with the cheap Art-furniture as before—
except that the candles on the Christmas tree have
guttered down and appear to have been lately
blown out. The cotton-wool frogs and the chenille
monkeys are disarranged, and there are walking
things on the sofa.* NORA *alone.*

NORA.

[*Putting on a cloak and taking it off again.*]
Bother Krogstad! There, I won't think of him.
I'll only think of the costume ball at Consul
Stenborg's, over-head, to-night, where I am to dance
the Tarantella all alone, dressed as a Capri fisher-

D

girl.   It struck Torvald that, as I am a matron with
three children, my performance might amuse the
Consul's guests, and, at the same time, increase his
connection at the Bank.   Torvald *is* so practical.
[*To* MRS. LINDEN, *who comes in with a large card-
board box.*] Ah, Christina, so you have brought in
my old costume?   *Would* you mind, as my husband's
new Cashier, just doing up the trimming for me?

MRS. LINDEN.

Not at all—is it not part of my regular duties?
[*Sewing.*] Don't you think, Nora, that you see a
little too much of Dr. Rank?

NORA.

Oh, I *couldn't* see too much of Dr. Rank! He *is*
so amusing—always talking about his complaints,
and heredity, and all sorts of indescribably funny
things.   Go away now, dear; I hear Torvald.

> [MRS. LINDEN *goes.   Enter* TORVALD *from
> the Manager's room.*   NORA *runs trip-
> pingly to him.*

NORA.

[*Coaxing.*] Oh, Torvald, if only you won't dismiss Krogstad, you can't think how your little lark would jump about and twitter.

HELMER.

The inducement would be stronger but for the fact that, as it is, the little lark is generally engaged in that particular occupation. And I really *must* get rid of Krogstad. If I didn't, people would say I was under the thumb of my little squirrel here, and then Krogstad and I knew each other in early youth; and when two people knew each other in early youth —[*a short pause*]—h'm! Besides, he *will* address me as, " I say, Torvald "—which causes me most painful emotion! He is tactless, dishonest, familiar, and morally ruined—altogether not at all the kind of person to be a Cashier in a Bank like mine.

NORA.

But he writes in scurrilous papers—he is on the staff of the Norwegian *Punch*. If you dismiss him, he may write nasty things about *you*, as wicked people did about poor dear papa!

Helmer.

Your poor dear papa was not impeccable—far from it. I *am*—which makes all the difference. I have here a letter giving Krogstad the sack. One of the conveniences of living close to the Bank is, that I can use the housemaids as Bank-messengers. [*Goes to door and calls.*] Ellen! [*Enter parlourmaid.*] Take that letter—there is no answer. [Ellen *takes it and goes.*] That's settled—and now, Nora, as I am going to my private room, it will be a capital opportunity for you to practise the tambourine—thump away, little lark, the doors are double!

[*Nods to her and goes in, shutting door.*

Nora.

[*Stroking her face.*] How *am* I to get out of this mess? [*A ring at the visitors' bell.*] Dr. Rank's ring!

"A poor fellow with both feet in the grave is not the best
authority on the fit of silk stockings."

He shall help me out of it ! [DR. RANK *appears in doorway, hanging up his great-coat.*] Dear Dr. Rank, how *are* you ?   [*Takes both his hands.*

DR. RANK.

[*Sitting down near the stove.*] I am a miserable, hypochondriacal wretch—that's what *I* am. And why am I doomed to be dismal ? Why ? Because my father died of a fit of the blues ! *Is* that fair—I put it to *you ?*

NORA.

Do try to be funnier than *that !* See, I will show you the flesh-coloured silk tights that I am to wear to-night—it will cheer you up. But you must only look at the feet—well, you may look at the rest if you're good. *Aren't* they lovely ? Will they fit me, do you think ?

DR. RANK.

[*Gloomily.*] A poor fellow with both feet in the grave is not the best authority on the fit of silk stockings. I shall be food for worms before long—I *know* I shall !

Nora.

You mustn't really be so frivolous! Take that!
[*She hits him lightly on the ear with the stockings;
then hums a little.*] I want you to do me a great
service, Dr. Rank. [*Rolling up stockings.*] I always
liked *you.* I love Torvald most, of *course*—but,
somehow, I'd rather spend my time with you—you
are so amusing !

Rank.

If I am, can't you guess why? [*A short silence.*]
Because I love you! You can't pretend you didn't
know it!

Nora.

Perhaps not—but it was really too clumsy of you
to mention it just as I was about to ask a favour of
you! It was in the worst taste! [*With dignity.*]
You must not imagine because I joke with you about
silk stockings, and tell you things I never tell Torvald,
that I am therefore without the most delicate and
scrupulous self-respect! I am really quite a good

little doll, Dr. Rank, and now—[*sits in rocking chair and smiles*]—now I shan't ask you what I was going to !   [ELLEN *comes in with a card.*]

NORA.

[*Terrified.*] Oh, my goodness !

> [*Puts it in her pocket.*

DR. RANK.

Excuse my easy Norwegian pleasantry—but—h'm —anything disagreeable up ?

NORA.

[*To herself.*] Krogstad's card ! I must tell *another* whopper ! [*To* RANK.] No, nothing—only—only my new costume. I want to try it on here. I always do try on my dresses in the drawing-room—it's *cosier*, you know. So go in to Torvald and amuse him till I'm ready.

> [RANK *goes into* HELMER'S *room, and* NORA *bolts the door upon him, as* KROGSTAD *enters from hall in a fur cap.*

Krogstad.

Well, I've got the sack, and so I came to see how *you* are getting on. I mayn't be a nice man, but— [*with feeling*]—I have a heart! And, as I don't intend to give up the forged I.O.U. unless I'm taken back, I was afraid you might be contemplating suicide, or something of that kind; and so I called to tell you that, if I were you, I wouldn't. Bad thing for the complexion, suicide—and silly, too, because it wouldn't mend matters in the least. [*Kindly.*] You must not take this affair too seriously, Mrs. Helmer. Get your husband to settle it amicably by taking me back as Cashier; *then* I shall soon get the whip-hand of *him*, and we shall all be as pleasant and comfortable as possible together!

Nora.

Not even that prospect can tempt me! Besides, Torvald wouldn't have you back at any price now!

Krogstad.

All right, then. I have here a letter, telling your husband all. I will take the liberty of dropping it in the letter-box at your hall-door as I go out. I'll wish you good evening !

> [*He goes out ; presently the dull sound of a thick letter dropping into a wire box is heard.*

Nora.

[*Softly, and hoarsely.*] He's done it ! How *am* I to prevent Torvald from seeing it ?

Helmer.

[*Inside the door, rattling.*] Hasn't my lark changed its dress yet ? [Nora *unbolts door.*] What—so you are *not* in fancy costume, after all ? [*Enters with* Rank.] Are there any letters for me in the box there ?

Nora.

[*Voicelessly.*] None—not even a postcard ! Oh,

Torvald, don't, please, go and look—*promise* me you won't! I do *assure* you there isn't a letter! And I've forgotten the Tarantella you taught me—do let's run over it. I'm so afraid of breaking down—promise me not to look at the letter-box. I can't dance unless you do.

HELMER.

[*Standing still, on his way to the letter-box.*] I am a man of strict business habits, and some powers of observation; my little squirrel's assurances that there is nothing in the box, combined with her obvious anxiety that I should not go and see for myself, satisfy me that it is indeed empty, in spite of the fact that I have not invariably found her a strictly truthful little dicky-bird. There—there. [*Sits down to piano.*] Bang away on your tambourine, little squirrel—dance away, my own lark!

NORA.

[*Dancing, with a long gay shawl.*] Just *won't* the little squirrel! Faster—faster! Oh, I *do* feel so gay! We will have some champagne for dinner, *won't* we, Torvald?

[*Dances with more and more abandonment.*

HELMER.

[*After addressing frequent remarks in correction.*]
Come, come—not this awful wildness! I don't like
to see *quite* such a larky little lark as this. . . . .
Really it is time you stopped!

NORA.

[*Her hair coming down as she dances more wildly
still, and swings the tambourine.*] I can't. I
can't! [*To herself, as she dances.*] I've only thirty-
one hours left to be a bird in; and after that—
[*shuddering*]—after *that*, Krogstad will let the cat
out of the bag!

Curtain.

ACT THIRD

The same room—except that the sofa has been slightly moved, and one of the Japanese cotton-wool frogs has fallen into the fire-place. MRS. LINDEN *sits and reads a book—but without understanding a single line.*

MRS. LINDEN.

[*Laying down her book, as a light tread is heard outside.*] Here he is at last! [KROGSTAD *comes in, and stands in the doorway.*] Mr. Krogstad, I have given you a secret *rendezvous* in this room, because it belongs to my employer, Mr. Helmer, who has lately discharged you. The etiquette of Norway permits these slight freedoms on the part of a female cashier.

Krogstad.

It does. Are we alone ? [Nora *is heard overhead dancing the Tarantella.*] Yes, I hear Mrs. Helmer's fairy footfall above. She dances the Tarantella now—by-and-by she will dance to another tune ! [*Changing his tone.*] I don't exactly know why you should wish to have this interview—after jilting me as you did, long ago, though ?

Mrs. Linden.

Don't you ? *I* do. I am a widow—a Norwegian widow. And it has occurred to me that there may be a nobler side to your nature somewhere—though you have not precisely the best of reputations

Krogstad.

Right. I am a forger, and a money-lender ; I am on the staff of the Norwegian *Punch*—a most scurrilous paper. More, I have been blackmailing

Mrs. Helmer by trading on her fears, like a low cowardly cur. But, in spite of all that—[*clasping his hands*]—there are the makin   of a fine man about me *yet*, Christina!

MRS. LINDEN.

I believe you—at least, I'll chance it. I want some one to care for, and I'll marry you.

KROGSTAD.

[*Suspiciously.*] On condition, I suppose, that I suppress the letter denouncing Mrs. Helmer?

MRS. LINDEN.

How can you think so? I am her dearest friend; but I can still see her faults, and it is my firm opinion that a sharp lesson will do her all the good in the world. She is *much* too comfortable. So leave the letter in the box, and come home with me.

KROGSTAD.

I am wildly happy! Engaged to the female

cashier of the manager who has discharged me, our
future is bright and secure !

> [*He goes out; and* Mrs. Linden *sets the
> furniture straight; presently a noise
> is heard outside, and* Helmer *enters,
> dragging* Nora *in. She is in fancy
> dress, and he in an open black domino.*

Nora.

I shan't ! It's too early to come away from such a
nice party. I *won't* go to bed ! [*She whimpers.*

Helmer.

[*Tenderly.*] There'sh a naughty lil' larkie for you,
Mrs. Linen ! Poshtively had to drag her 'way !
She'sh a capricious lil' girl—from Capri. 'Scuse me !
—'fraid I've been and made a pun. Shan' 'cur
again ! Shplendid champagne the Consul gave us—
'counts for it ! [*Sits down smiling.*] Do you *knit,*
Mrs. Cotton ? . . . . You shouldn't. Never knit.
'Broider. [*Nodding to her, solemnly.*] 'Member that.

E

Alwaysh *'broider.* More—[*hiccoughing*] — Oriental !
Gobblesh you !—goo'ni !

MRS. LINDEN.

I only came in to— to see Nora's costume. Now
I've seen it, I'll go.   [*Goes out.*

HELMER.

Awful bore that woman—hate boresh ! [*Looks at*
NORA, *then comes nearer.*] Oh, you prillil squillikins,
I *do* love you so ! Shomehow, I feel sho lively
thishevenin' !

NORA.

[*Goes to other side of table.*] I won't *hare* all that,
Torvald !

HELMER.

Why ? ain't you my lil' lark—ain't thish our lil
cage ? Ver-*well,* then. [*A ring.*] Rank ! confound
it all ! [*Enter* Dr. RANK.] Rank, dear old boy,
you've been [*hiccoughs*] going it upstairs. Cap'tal
champagne, eh ? '*Shamed* of you, Rank !

[*He sits down on sofa, and closes his eyes gently.*

"Oh, you prillil squillikins!"

Dr. Rank.

Did you notice it? [*With pride.*] It was almost incredible the amount I contrived to put away. But I shall suffer for it to-morrow. [*Gloomily.*] Heredity again! I wish I was dead! I do.

Nora.

Don't apologise. Torvald was just as bad; but he is always so good-tempered after champagne.

Doctor Rank.

Ah, well, I just looked in to say that I haven't long to live. Don't weep for me, Mrs. Helmer, it's chronic—and hereditary too. Here are my P.P.C. cards. I'm a fading flower. Can you oblige me with a cigar?

Nora.

[*With a suppressed smile.*] Certainly. Let me give you a light?

> [DOCTOR RANK *lights his cigar, after several
> ineffectual attempts, and goes out.*

HELMER.

[*Compassionately.*] Poo' old Rank—he'sh very bad to-ni'! [*Pulls himself together.*] But I forgot— Bishness—I mean, bu-si-ness—mush be 'tended to. I'll go and see if there are any letters. [*Goes to box.*] Hallo! some one's been at the lock with a hairpin— it's one of *your* hairpins! [*Holding it out to her.*

NORA.

[*Quickly.*] Not mine—one of Bob's, or Ivar's— they both wear hairpins!

HELMER.

[*Turning over letters absently.*] You must break them of it—bad habit! What a lot o' lettersh! *double* usual quantity. [*Opens* KROGSTAD'S.] By Jove! [*Reads it and falls back completely sobered.*] What have you got to say to *this*?

NORA.

[*Crying aloud.*] You shan't save me—let me go! I *won't* be saved!

HELMER.

Save *you*, indeed ! Who's going to save *Me ?* You
miserable little criminal. [*Annoyed.*] Ugh—ugh !

NORA.

[*With hardening expression.*] Indeed, Torvald, your
singing-bird acted for the best !

HELMER.

Singing-bird ! Your father was a rook—and you
take *after* him. Heredity again ! You have utterly
destroyed my happiness. [*Walks round several times.*]
Just as I was beginning to get on, too !

NORA.

I have—but I will go away and jump into the
water.

HELMER.

What good will *that* do me ? People will say *I* had
a hand in this business. [*Bitterly.*] If you *must* forge,
you might at least put your dates in correctly ! But
you never *had* any principle ! [*A ring.*] The front-

door bell ! [*A fat letter is seen to fall into the box ;* HELMER *takes it, opens it, sees enclosure, and embraces* NORA.] Krogstad won't split. See, he returns the forged I.O.U.! Oh, my poor little lark, *what* you must have gone through ! Come under my wing, my little scared song-bird. . . . . Eh? you *won't !* Why, what's the matter *now ?*

NORA.

[*With cold calm.*] I have wings of my own, thank you, Torvald, and I mean to use them !

HELMER.

What—leave your pretty cage, and [*pathetically*] the old cock bird, and the poor little innocent eggs !

NORA.

Exactly. Sit down, and we will talk it over first. [*Slowly.*] Has it ever struck you that this is the first time you and I have ever talked seriously together about serious things ?

HELMER.

Come, I do like that! How on earth could we talk about serious things when your mouth was always full of macaroons?

NORA.

[*Shakes her head.*] Ah, Torvald, the mouth of a mother of a family should have more solemn things in it than macaroons! I see that now, too late. No, you have wronged me. So did papa. Both of you called me a doll, and a squirrel, and a lark! You might have made something of me—and instead of that, you went and made too much of me—oh, you *did !*

HELMER.

Well, you didn't seem to object to it, and really I don't exactly see what it is you *do* want !

NORA.

No more do I—that is what I have got to find out. If I had been properly educated, I should have known better than to date poor papa's signature three days after he died. Now I must educate *myself*. I have to gain experience, and get clear about religion, and law, and things, and whether Society is right or I am—and I must go away and never come back any more till I *am* educated!

HELMER.

Then you may be away some little time? And what's to become of me and the eggs meanwhile?

NORA.

That, Torvald, is entirely your own affair. I have a higher duty than that towards you and the eggs. [*Looking solemnly upward.*] I mean my duty towards Myself!

HELMER.

And all this because—in a momentary annoyance at finding myself in the power of a discharged cashier who calls me "I say, Torvald," I expressed myself with ultra-Gilbertian frankness! You talk like a silly child!

Nora.

Because my eyes are opened, and I see my position with the eyes of Ibsen. I must go away at once, and begin to educate myself.

Helmer.

May I ask how you are going to set about it?

Nora.

Certainly. I shall begin—yes, I shall *begin* with a course of the Norwegian theatres. If *that* doesn't take the frivolity out of me, I don't really know what *will!*   [*She gets her bonnet and ties it tightly.*

Helmer.

Then you are really going? And you'll never think about me and the eggs any more! Oh, Nora!

Nora.

Indeed, I shall—occasionally—as strangers.

> [*She puts on a shawl sadly, and fetches her dressing-bag.*]

If I ever do come back, the greatest miracle of all
will have to happen.   Good-bye!

> [*She goes out through the hall ; the front door
> is heard to bang loudly.*

HELMER.

[*Sinking on a chair.*] The room empty?   Then she
must be gone!   Yes, my little lark has flown! [*The
dull sound of an unskilled latchkey is heard trying
the lock ; presently the door opens, and* NORA, *with a
somewhat foolish expression, reappears.*] What? back
already!   Then you *are* educated?

NORA.

[*Puts down dressing-bag.*] No, Torvald, not yet.
Only, you see, I found I had only threepence-half-
penny in my purse, and the Norwegian theatres are
all closed at this hour—and so I thought I wouldn't
leave the cage till to-morrow—after breakfast.

HELMER.

[*As if to himself.*] The greatest miracle of all *has*

happened. My little bird is not in the bush *just* yet!

> [NORA *takes down a showily-bound diction-*
> *ary from the shelf and begins her educa-*
> *tion ;* HELMER *fetches a bag of macaroons,*
> *sits near her, and tenders one humbly. A*
> *pause.* NORA *repulses it, proudly. He*
> *offers it again. She snatches at it sud-*
> *denly, still without looking at him, and*
> *nibbles it thoughtfully as Curtain falls.*

HEDDA GABLER

HEDDA GABLER

ACT FIRST

SCENE—*A sitting-room cheerfully decorated in dark colours. Broad doorway, hung with black crape, in the wall at back, leading to a back drawing-room, in which, above a sofa in black horsehair, hangs a posthumous portrait of the late* GENERAL GABLER. *On the piano is a handsome pall. Through the glass panes of the back drawing-room window are seen a dead wall and a cemetery. Settees, sofas, chairs, &c., handsomely upholstered in black bombazine, and studded with small round nails. Bouquets of immortelles and dead grasses are lying everywhere about.*

F

Enter AUNT JULIE (*a good-natured-looking lady
in a smart hat.*)

AUNT JULIE.

Well, I declare, if I believe George or Hedda are
up yet! [*Enter* GEORGE TESMAN, *humming, stout,
careless, spectacled.*] Ah, my dear boy, I have called
before breakfast to inquire how you and Hedda are
after returning late last night from your long honeymoon. Oh, dear me, yes; am I not your old aunt,
and are not these attentions usual in Norway?

GEORGE.

Good Lord, yes! My six months' honeymoon
has been quite a little travelling scholarship, eh? I
have been examining archives. Think of *that!* Look
here, I'm going to write a book all about the
domestic interests of the Cave-dwellers during the
Deluge. I'm a clever young Norwegian man of
letters, eh?

AUNT JULIE.

Fancy your knowing about that too! Now, dear me, thank Heaven!

GEORGE.

Let me, as a dutiful Norwegian nephew, untie that smart, showy hat of yours. [*Unties it, and pats her under the chin.*] Well, to be sure, you have got yourself really up—fancy that!

[*He puts hat on chair close to table.*

AUNT JULIE.

[*Giggling.*] It was for Hedda's sake—to go out walking with her in. [HEDDA *approaches from the back-room; she is pallid, with cold, open, steel-grey eyes; her hair is not very thick, but what there is of it is an agreeable medium brown.*] Ah, dear Hedda!

[*She attempts to cuddle her.*

HEDDA.

[*Shrinking back.*] Ugh, let me go, do! [*Looking at* AUNT JULIE'S *hat.*] Tesman, you must really tell the housemaid not to leave her old hat about on the drawing-room chairs. Oh, is it *your* hat? Sorry I spoke, I'm sure!

AUNT JULIE.

[*Annoyed.*] Good gracious, little Mrs. Hedda; my nice new hat that I bought to go out walking with *you* in!

GEORGE.

[*Patting her on the back.*] Yes, Hedda, she did, and the parasol too! Fancy, Aunt Julie always positively thinks of everything, eh?

HEDDA.

[*Coldly.*] You hold *your* tongue. Catch me going out walking with your aunt! One doesn't *do* such things.

GEORGE.

[*Beaming.*] Isn't she a charming woman? Such fascinating manners! My goodness, eh? Fancy that!

Aunt Julie.

Ah, dear George, you ought indeed to be happy—
but [*brings out a flat package wrapped in newspaper*]
look *here*, my dear boy!

George.

[*Opens it.*] What? my dear old morning shoes!
my slippers! [*Breaks down.*] This is positively too
touching, Hedda, eh? Do you remember how badly
I wanted them all the honeymoon? Come and just
have a look at them—you *may!*

Hedda.

Bother your old slippers and your old aunt too!
[Aunt Julie *goes out annoyed, followed by* George,
still thanking her warmly for the slippers; Hedda
yawns; George *comes back and places his old slippers
reverently on the table.*] Why, here comes Mrs
Elvsted—*another* early caller! She had irritating

hair, and went about making a sensation with it—
an old flame of yours, I've heard.

Enter Mrs. Elvsted; *she is pretty and gentle, with
copious wavy white-gold hair and round promi-
nent eyes, and the manner of a frightened rabbit.*

Mrs. Elvsted.

[*Nervous.*] Oh, please, I'm so perfectly in despair.
Ejlert Lövborg, you know, who was our tutor; he's
written such a large new book. I inspired him. Oh,
I know I don't look like it—but I did—he told me
so. And, good gracious! now he's in this dangerous
wicked town all alone, and he's a reformed character,
and I'm *so* frightened about him; so, as the wife of a
sheriff twenty years older than me, I came up to
look after Mr. Lövborg. Do ask him here—then I
can meet him. You will? How perfectly lovely of
you! My husband's *so* fond of him!

Hedda.

George, go and write an invitation at once; do you
hear? [George *looks around for his slippers, takes*

them up and goes out.] Now we can talk, my little Thea. Do you remember how I used to pull your hair when we met on the stairs, and say I would scorch it off? Seeing people with copious hair always *does* irritate me.

Mrs. Elvsted.

Goodness, yes, you were always so playful and friendly, and I was so afraid of you. I am still. And please, I've run away from my husband. Everything around him was distasteful to me. And Mr. Lövborg and I were comrades—he was dissipated, and I got a sort of power over him, and he made a real person out of me—which I wasn't before, you know; but, oh, I do hope I'm real now. He talked to me and taught me to think—chiefly of him. So, when Mr. Lövborg came here, naturally I came too. There was nothing else to do! And fancy, there is another woman whose shadow still stands between him and me! She wanted to shoot him once, and so, of course, he can never forget her. I wish I knew her name—perhaps it was that red-haired opera-singer?

HEDDA.

[*With cold self-command.*] Very likely—but nobody does that sort of thing here. Hush! Run away now. Here comes Tesman with Judge Brack. [MRS. ELVSTED *goes out;* GEORGE *comes in with* JUDGE BRACK, *who is a short and elastic gentleman, with a round face, carefully brushed hair, and distinguished profile.*] How awfully funny you do look by daylight, Judge!

BRACK.

[*Holding his hat and dropping his eye-glass.*] Sincerest thanks. Still the same graceful manners, dear little Mrs. Hed—Tesman! I came to invite dear Tesman to a little bachelor-party to celebrate his return from his long honeymoon. It is customary in Scandinavian society. It will be a lively affair, for I am a gay Norwegian dog.

"I am a gay Norwegian dog."

GEORGE.

Asked out—without my wife! Think of that! Eh? Oh, dear me, yes, *I'll* come!

BRACK.

By the way, Lövborg is here; he has written a wonderful book, which has made a quite extraordinary sensation. Bless me, yes!

GEORGE.

Lövborg—fancy! Well, I *am*—glad. Such marvellous gifts! And I was so painfully certain he had gone to the bad. Fancy that, eh? But what will become of him *now*, poor fellow, eh? I *am* so anxious to know!

BRACK.

Well, he may possibly put up for the Professorship against you, and, though you *are* an uncommonly clever man of letters—for a Norwegian—it's not wholly improbable that he may cut you out!

GEORGE.

But, look here, good Lord, Judge Brack!—[*gesticulating*]—that would show an incredible want of consideration for me! I married on my chance of *getting* that professorship. A man like Lövborg, too, who hasn't even been respectable, eh? One doesn't do such things as that!

BRACK.

Really? You forget we are all realistic and unconventional persons here, and do all kinds of odd things. But don't worry yourself!   [*He goes out.*

GEORGE.

[*To* HEDDA.] Oh, I say, Hedda, what's to become of our fairyland now, eh? We can't have a liveried servant, or give dinner parties, or have a horse for riding. Fancy that!

HEDDA.

[*Slowly, and wearily.*] No, we shall really have to set up as fairies in reduced circumstances, now.

GEORGE.

[*Cheering up.*] Still, we shall see Aunt Julie every day, and *that* will be something, and I've got back my old slippers. We shan't be altogether without some amusements, eh?

HEDDA.

[*Crosses the floor.*] Not while I have *one* thing to amuse myself with, at all events.

GEORGE.

[*Beaming with joy.*] Oh, Heaven be praised and thanked for that! My goodness, so you have! And what may *that* be, Hedda, eh?

HEDDA.

[*At the doorway, with suppressed scorn.*] Yes, George you have the old slippers of the attentive aunt, and I have the horse-pistols of the deceased general!

GEORGE.

[*In an agony.*] The pistols! Oh, my goodness! *what* pistols?

Hedda.

[*With cold eyes.*] General Gabler's pistols—same which I shot—[*recollecting herself*]—no, that's Thackeray, not Ibsen—a *very* different person.

[*She goes through the back drawing-room.*

George.

[*At doorway, shouting after her.*] Dearest Hedda, *not* those dangerous things, eh? Why, they have never once been known to shoot straight yet! Don't! Have a catapult. For *my* sake, have a catapult!

[*Curtain.*

ACT SECOND

Scene—*The cheerful dark drawing-room. It is afternoon. Hedda stands loading a revolver in the
back drawing-room.*

Hedda.

[*Looking out and shouting.*] How do you do, Judge?
[*Aims at him.*] Mind yourself!   [*She fires.*

Brack.

[*Entering.*] What the devil! Do you usually take
pot-shots at casual visitors?   [*Annoyed.*

Hedda.

Invariably, when they come by the back-garden.
It is my unconventional way of intimating that I am

at home. One does do these things in realistic dramas,
you know. And I was only aiming at the blue sky.

BRACK.

Which accounts for the condition of my hat.
[*Exhibiting it.*] Look here—*riddled !*

HEDDA.

Couldn't help myself. I am so horribly bored with
Tesman. Everlastingly to be with a professional
person !

BRACK.

[*Sympathetically.*] Our excellent Tesman is certainly
a bit of a bore. [*Looks searchingly at her.*] What on
earth made you marry him ?

HEDDA.

Tired of dancing, my dear, that's all. And then I
used Tesman to take me home from parties; and we
saw this villa; and I said I liked it, and so did he;
and so we found some common ground, and here we

are, do you see! And I loathe Tesman, and I don't even like the villa now; and I do feel the want of an entertaining companion so!

BRACK.

Try me. Just the kind of three-cornered arrangement that I like. Let me be the third person in the compartment—[*confidentially*]—the tried friend, and, generally speaking, cock of the walk!

HEDDA.

[*Audibly drawing in her breath.*] I cannot resist your polished way of putting things. We will conclude a triple alliance. But hush!—here comes Tesman.

Enter GEORGE *with a number of books under his arm.*

GEORGE.

Puff! I *am* hot, HEDDA. I've been looking into Lövborg's new book. Wonderfully thoughtful— confound him! But I must go and dress for your party, Judge. [*He goes out.*

HEDDA.

I wish I could get Tesman to take to politics, Judge.
Couldn't he be a Cabinet Minister, or something?

BRACK.

H'm!

> [*A short pause; both look at one another,
> without speaking. Enter* GEORGE, *in
> evening dress with gloves.*

GEORGE.

It is afternoon, and your party is at half-past seven
—but I like to dress early. Fancy that! And I am
expecting Lövborg.

> EJLERT LÖVBORG *comes in from the hall; he is worn
> and pale, with red patches on his cheek-bones, and
> wears an elegant perfectly new visiting-suit and
> black gloves.*

GEORGE.

Welcome! [*Introduces him to* BRACK.] Listen—I
have got your new book, but I haven't read it through
yet.

Lövborg.

You needn't—it's rubbish. [*Takes a packet of MSS. out.*] This *isn't*. It's in three parts; the first about the civilising forces of the future, the second about the future of the civilising forces, and the third about the forces of the future civilisation. I thought I'd read you a little of it this evening?

Brack *and* George.

[*Hastily.*] Awfully nice of you—but there's a little party this evening—so sorry we can't stop! Won't you come too?

Hedda.

No, he must stop and read it to me and Mrs. Elvsted instead.

George.

It would never have occurred to me to think of such clever things! Are you going to oppose me for the professorship, eh?

LÖVBORG.

[*Modestly.*] No; I shall only triumph over you in the popular judgment—that's all !

GEORGE.

Oh, is that all ?　Fancy !　Let us go into the back drawing-room and drink cold punch.

LÖVBORG.

Thanks—but I am a reformed character, and have renounced cold punch—it is poison.

> [GEORGE *and* BRACK *go into the back-room*
> *and drink punch, whilst* HEDDA *shows*
> LÖVBORG *a photograph album in the front.*

LÖVBORG.

[*Slowly, in a low tone.*] Hedda Gabbler ! how *could* you throw yourself away like this !—Oh, is *that* the Ortler Group ?　Beautiful !——Have you forgotten how we used to sit on the settee together behind an illustrated paper, and—yes, very picturesque peaks— I told you all about how I had been on the loose ?

HEDDA.

Now, none of that here! These are the Dolomites. —Yes, I remember; it was a beautiful fascinating Norwegian intimacy—but it's over now. See, we spent a night in that little mountain village, Tesman and I.

LÖVBORG.

Did you, indeed? Do you remember that delicious moment when you threatened to shoot me down? [*Tenderly*] I do!

HEDDA.

[*Carelessly.*] Did I! I have done that to so many people. But now all that is past, and you have found the loveliest consolation in dear, good, little Mrs. Elvsted—ah, here she is! [*Enter* MRS. ELVSTED.] Now, Thea, sit down and drink up a good glass of cold punch. Mr. Lövborg is going to have some. If you don't, Mr. Lövborg, George and the Judge will think you are afraid of taking too much if you once begin.

MRS. ELVSTED.

Oh, please, Hedda! When I've inspired Mr.
Lövborg so—good gracious! *don't* make him drink
cold punch!

HEDDA.

You see, Mr. Lövborg, our dear little friend can't
trust you!

LÖVBORG.

So *that* is my comrade's faith in me! [*Gloomily.*]
I'll show her if I am to be trusted or not. [*He drinks
a glass of punch.*] Now I'll go to the Judge's party
I'll have another glass first. Your health, Thea!
So you came up to spy on me, eh? I'll drink the
Sheriff's health—*everybody's* health!

[*He tries to get more punch.*

HEDDA.

[*Stopping him.*] No more now. You are going to
a party, remember.

GEORGE *and* TESMAN *come in from back-room.*

Lövborg.

Don't be angry, Thea. I was fallen for a moment. Now I'm up again! [Mrs. Elsted *beams with delight.*] Judge, I'll come to your party, as you *are* so pressing, and I'll read George my manuscript all the evening. I'll do all in *my* power to make that party go!

George.

No? fancy! that *will* be amusing!

Hedda.

There, go away, you wild rollicking creatures! But Mr. Lövborg must be back at ten, to take dear Thea home!

Mrs. Elvsted.

Oh, goodness, yes! [*In concealed agony.*] Mr. Lövborg, I shan't go away till you do!

> [*The three men go out laughing merrily; the Act-drop is lowered for a minute; when it is raised, it is 7 A.M., and* Mrs. Elvsted *and* Hedda *are discovered sitting up, with rugs around them.*

MRS. ELVSTED

[*Wearily.*] Seven in the morning, and Mr. Lövborg not here to take me home *yet!* what *can* he be doing?

HEDDA.

[*Yawning.*] Reading to Tesman, with vine-leaves in his hair, I suppose. Perhaps he has got to the third part.

MRS. ELVSTED.

Oh, do you *really* think so, Hedda. Oh, if I could but hope he was doing that!

HEDDA.

You silly little ninny! I should like to scorch your hair off. Go to bed!

[MRS. ELVSTED *goes. Enter* GEORGE.

GEORGE.

I'm a little late, eh? But we made *such* a night of it. Fancy! It was most amusing. Ejlert read his book to me—think of that! Astonishing book!

Oh, we really had great fun ! I wish *I'd* written it. Pity he's so irreclaimable.

HEDDA.

I suppose you mean he has more of the courage of life than most people ?

GEORGE.

Good Lord! He had the courage to get more drunk than most people. But, altogether, it was what you might almost call a Bacchanalian orgy. We finished up by going to have early coffee with some of these jolly chaps, and poor old Lövborg dropped his precious manuscript in the mud, and I picked it up—and here it is! Fancy if anything were to happen to it! He never could write it again. *Wouldn't* it be sad, eh ? Don't tell any one about it.

> [*He leaves the packet of MSS. on a chair,
> and rushes out ;* HEDDA *hides the packet
> as* BRACK *enters.*

Brack.

Another early call, you see! My party was such a singularly animated *soirée* that I haven't undressed all night. Oh, it was the liveliest affair conceivable! And, like a true Norwegian host, I tracked Lövborg home; and it is only my duty, as a friend of the house, and cock of the walk, to take the first opportunity of telling you that he finished up the evening by coming to mere loggerheads with a red-haired opera-singer, and being taken off to the police-station! Your mustn't have him here any more. Remember our little triple alliance!

Hedda.

[*Her smile fading away.*] You are certainly a dangerous person—but you must not get a hold over *me!*

Brack.

[*Ambiguously.*] What an idea! But I might—I am an insinuating dog. Good morning! [*Goes out.*

LÖVBORG.

[*Bursting in, confused and excited.*] I suppose you've heard where *I've* been ?

HEDDA.

[*Evasively.*] I heard you had a very jolly party at Judge Brack's.

MRS. ELVSTED *comes in.*

LÖVBORG.

It's all over. I don't mean to do any more work. I've no use for a companion now, Thea. Go home to your sheriff !

MRS. ELVSTED.

[*Agitated.*] Never ! I want to be with you when your book comes out !

LÖVBORG.

It won't *come* out—I've torn it up ! [MRS. ELSTED *rushes out, wringing her hands.*] Mrs. Tesman, I told her a lie—but no matter. I haven't torn my book up—I've done worse ! I've taken it about to several

parties, and it's been through a police-row with me—
now I've lost it. Even if I found it again, it wouldn't
be the same—not to me! I am a Norwegian literary
man, and peculiar. So I must make an end of it
altogether!

HEDDA.

Quite so—but look here, you must do it beautifully. I don't insist on your putting vine-leaves in
your hair—but do it beautifully. [*Fetches pistol.*]
See, here is one of General Gabler's pistols—do it
with *that !*

LÖVBORG.

Thanks!

> [*He takes the pistol, and goes out through the
> hall-door; as soon as he has gone,* HEDDA
> *brings out the manuscript, and puts it on
> the fire, whispering to herself, as Curtain
> falls.*

"I am a Norwegian literary man, and peculiar."

ACT THREE

Scene.—*The same room, but—it being evening—darker than ever. The crape curtains are drawn. A servant, with black ribbons in her cap, and red eyes, comes in and lights the gas quietly and carefully. Chords are heard on the piano in the back drawing-room. Presently* Hedda *comes in and looks out into the darkness. A short pause. Enter* George Tesman.

George.

I am so uneasy about poor Lövborg. Fancy! he is not at home. Mrs. Elvsted told me he has been here early this morning, so I suppose you gave him back his manuscript, eh?

HEDDA.

[*Cold and immovable, supported by arm-chair.*] No, I put it on the fire instead.

GEORGE.

On the fire! Lövborg's wonderful new book that he read to me at Brack's party, when we had that wild revelry last night! Fancy *that!* But, I say, Hedda—isn't that *rather*—eh? *Too* bad, you know —really. A great work like that. How on earth did you come to think of it?

HEDDA.

[*Suppressing an almost imperceptible smile.*] Well, dear George, you gave me a tolerably strong hint.

GEORGE.

Me? Well, to be sure—that *is* a joke! Why, I only said that I envied him for writing such a book, and it would put me entirely in the shade if it came out, and if anything was to happen to it, I should

never forgive myself, as poor Lövborg couldn't write
it all over again, and so we must take the greatest
care of it! And then I left it on a chair and went
away—that was all! And you went and burnt the
book all up! Bless me, who *would* have expected it?

HEDDA.

Nobody, you dear simple old soul! But I did it
for your sake—it was *love*, George!

GEORGE.

[*In an outburst between doubt and joy.*] Hedda, you
don't mean that! Your love takes such queer forms
sometimes. Yes, but yes—[*laughing in excess of joy*]
why, you *must* be fond of me! Just think of that
now! Well, you *are* fun, Hedda! Look here, I must
just run and tell the housemaid that—she will enjoy
the joke so, eh?

HEDDA.

[*Coldly, in self-command.*] It is surely not necessary
even for a clever Norwegian man of letters in a

II

realistic social drama, to make quite such a fool of himself as all that?

GEORGE.

No, that's true too. Perhaps we'd better keep it quiet—though I *must* tell Aunt Julie—it will make her so happy to hear that you burnt a manuscript on my account! And, besides, I should like to ask her whether that's a usual thing with young wives. [*Looks uneasy and pensive again.*] But poor old Ejlert's manuscript! Oh Lor', you know! Well, well!

MRS. ELVSTED *comes in*

MRS. ELVSTED.

Oh, please, I'm so uneasy about dear Mr. Lövborg. Something has happened to him, I'm sure!

[JUDGE BRACK *comes in from the hall, with a new hat in his hand.*

BRACK.

You have guessed it, first time. Something *has!*

Mrs. Elvsted.

Oh, dear, good gracious! What is it? Something distressing, I'm certain of it! [*Shrieks aloud.*

Brack.

[*Pleasantly.*] That depends on how one takes it. He has shot himself, and is in a hospital now, that's all!

George.

[*Sympathetically.*] That's sad, eh? poor old Lövborg! Well, I *am* cut up to hear that. Fancy, though, eh?

Hedda.

Was it through the temple, or through the breast? The breast? Well, one can do it beautifully through the breast, too, Do you know, as an advanced woman, I like an act of that sort—it's so positive to have the courage to settle the account with himself—it's beautiful, really!

Mrs. Elvsted.

Oh, Hedda, what an odd way to look at it! But never mind poor dear Mr. Lövborg now. What *we've*

got to do is to see if we can't put his wonderful
manuscript, that he said he had torn to pieces, together
again. [*Takes a bundle of small pages out of the pocket
of her mantle.*] There are the loose scraps he dictated
it to me from. I hid them on the chance of some
such emergency. And if dear Mr. Tesman and I
were to put our heads together, I *do* think something
might come of it.

GEORGE.

Fancy! I will dedicate my life—or all I can spare
of it—to the task. I seem to feel I owe him some
slight amends, perhaps. No use crying over spilt
milk, eh, Mrs. Elvsted? We'll sit down—just you
and I—in the back drawing-room, and see if you can't
inspire me as you did him, eh?

MRS. ELVSTED.

Oh, goodness, yes! I should like it—if it only might
be possible!

[GEORGE *and* MRS. ELVSTED *go into the back
drawing-room and become absorbed in*

*eager conversation; HEDDA sits in a chair
in the front room, and a little later BRACK
crosses over to her*

HEDDA.

[*In a low tone.*] Oh, Judge, *what* a relief to know
that everything—including Lövborg's pistol—went off
so well! In the breast! Isn't there a veil of un-
intentional beauty in that? Such an act of voluntary
courage, too!

BRACK.

[*Smiles.*] H'm!—perhaps, dear Mrs. Hedda——

HEDDA.

[*Enthusiastically.*] But *wasn't* it sweet of him! To
have the courage to live his own life after his own
fashion—to break away from the banquet of life—*so*
early and *so* drunk! A beautiful act like that *does*
appeal to a superior woman's imagination!

BRACK.

Sorry to shatter your poetical illusions, little Mrs.
Hedda, but, as a matter of fact, our lamented friend

met his end under other circumstances. The shot did
not strike him in the *breast*—but——   [*Pauses.*

HEDDA.

[*Excitedly.*] General Gabler's pistols! I might have
known it! Did they *ever* shoot straight? Where
was he hit, then?

BRACK.

[*In a discreet undertone.*] A little lower down!

HEDDA.

Oh, *how* disgusting!—how vulgar!—how ridiculous!
—like everything else about me!

BRACK.

Yes, we're realistic types of human nature, and all
that—but a trifle squalid, perhaps. And why did you
give Lövborg your pistol, when it was certain to be
traced by the police? For a charming cold-blooded
woman with a clear head and no scruples, wasn't it
just a leetle foolish!

HEDDA.

Perhaps; but I wanted him to do it beautifully, and he didn't! Oh, I've just admitted that I *did* give him the pistol—how annoyingly unwise of me! Now I'm in *your* power, I suppose?

BRACK.

Precisely—for some reason it's not easy to understand. But it's inevitable, and you know how you dread anything approaching scandal. All your past proceedings show that. [*To* GEORGE *and* MRS. ELVSTED *who come in together from the back-room.*] Well, how are you getting on with the reconstruction of poor Lövborg's great work, eh?

GEORGE.

Capitally; we've made out the first two parts already. And really, Hedda, I do believe Mrs. Elvsted *is* inspiring me; I begin to feel it coming on. Fancy that!

Mrs. Elvsted.

Yes, goodness ! Hedda, *won't* it be lovely if I can. I mean to try *so* hard !

Hedda.

Do, you dear little silly rabbit; and while you are trying I will go into the back drawing-room and lie down.

> [*She goes into the back room and draws the curtains. Short pause. Suddenly she is heard playing* "The Bogie Man" *within on the piano.*

George.

But, dearest Hedda, don't play "*The Bogie Man*" this evening. As one of my aunts is dead, and poor old Lövborg has shot himself, it seems just a little pointed, eh ?

Hedda.

[*Puts her head out between the curtains.*] All right.

" What! the accounts of all those everlasting bores settled ? '

I'll be quiet after this. I'm going to practise with the late General Gabler's pistol!

> [*Closes the curtains again;* GEORGE *gets behind the stove,* JUDGE BRACK *under the table, and* MRS. ELVSTED *under the sofa. A shot is heard within.*

GEORGE.

[*Behind the stove.*] Eh, look here, I tell you what — she's hit *me !* Think of that!

> [*His legs are visibly agitated for a short time. Another shot is heard.*

MRS. ELVSTED.

[*Under the sofa.*] Oh, please, not me! Oh, goodness, now I can't inspire anybody any more. Oh !

> [*Her feet, which can be seen under the valance, quiver a little and then are suddenly still.*

BRACK.

[*Vivaciously, from under the table.*] I say, Mrs. Hedda, I'm coming in every evening—we will have great fun here togeth—— [*Another shot is heard.*] Bless me! to bring down the poor old cock-of-the-walk—it's unsportsmanlike!—people don't *do* such things as that!

> [*The table-cloth is violently agitated for a minute, and presently the curtains open, and* HEDDA *appears.*

HEDDA.

[*Clearly and firmly.*] I've been trying in there to shoot myself beautifully—but with General Gabler's pistol—[*She lifts the tablecloth, then looks behind the stove and under the sofa.*] What! the accounts of all those everlasting bores settled? Then my suicide becomes unnecessary. Yes, I feel the courage of life once more!

> [*She goes into the back-room and plays* "The Funeral March of a Marionette" *as the Curtain falls.*]

THE WILD DUCK

THE WILD DUCK

ACT FIRST

At WERLE'S *house. In front a richly-upholstered study.
(R.) A green baize door leading to* WERLE'S *office.
At back, open folding doors, revealing an elegant
dining-room, in which a brilliant Norwegian
dinner-party is going on. Hired Waiters in pro-
fusion. A glass is tapped with a knife. Shouts
of "Bravo!" Old* Mr. WERLE *is heard making
a long speech, proposing—according to the custom
of Norwegian society on such occasions—the health
of his Housekeeper,* Mrs. SÖRBY. *Presently
several short-sighted, flabby, and thin-haired*

CHAMBERLAINS *enter from the dining-room with*
HIALMAR EKDAL, *who writhes shyly under their
remarks.*

A CHAMBERLAIN.

As we are the sole surviving specimens of Norwegian nobility, suppose we sustain our reputation as
aristocratic sparklers by enlarging upon the enormous
amount we have eaten, and chaffing Hialmar Ekdal,
the friend of our host's son, for being a professional
photographer?

THE OTHER CHAMBERLAINS.

Bravo!   We will.

> [*They do; delight of* HIALMAR.   Old WERLE
> *comes in, leaning on his Housekeeper's
> arm, followed by his son,* GREGERS
> WERLE.

OLD WERLE.

[*Dejectedly.*]   Thirteen at table!   [*To* GREGERS,
with a meaning glance at HIALMAR.]   This is the

result of inviting an old college friend who has turned photographer! Wasting vintage wines on *him*, indeed.   [*He passes on gloomily.*

HIALMAR.

[*To* GREGERS.] I am almost sorry I came. Your old min is *not* friendly. Yet he set me up as a photographer fifteen years ago. *Now* he takes me down! But for him, I should never have married Gina, who, you may remember, was a servant in your family once.

GREGERS.

What? my old college friend married fifteen years ago—and to our Gina, of all people! If I had not been up at the works all these years, I suppose I should have heard something of such an event. But my father never mentioned it. Odd!

> [*He ponders;* OLD EKDAL *comes out through the green baize-door, bowing, and begging pardon, carrying copying work.* OLD

I

WERLE *says* "*Ugh*" *and* "*Pah*" *involuntarily.* HIALMAR *shrinks back, and looks another way.* A CHAMBERLAIN *asks him pleasantly if he knows that old man.*

HIALMAR.

I—oh no. Not in the least. No relation !

GREGERS.

[*Shocked.*] What, Hialmar, you, with your great soul, deny your own father !

HIALMAR.

[*Vehemently.*] Of course—what else *can* a photographer do with a disreputable old parent, who has been in a penitentiary for making a fraudulent map ? I shall leave this splendid banquet. The Chamberlains are not kind to me, and I feel the crushing hand of fate on my head !

[*Goes out hastily, feeling it.*

"Father, a word with you in private:
I loathe you."

MRS. SÖRBY.

[*Archly.*] Any nobleman here say " Cold Punch " ?
[*Every nobleman says " Cold Punch " and
follows her out in search of it with enthusiasm.* GREGERS *approaches his father,
who wishes he would go.*

GREGERS.

Father, a word with you in private. I loathe you.
I am nothing if not candid. Old Ekdal was your
partner once, and it's my firm belief you deserved a
prison quite as much as he did. However, you surely
need not have married our Gina to my old friend
Hialmar. You know very well she was no better than
she should have been !

OLD WERLE.

True—but then no more is Mrs. Sörby. And *I*
am going to marry *her*—if you have no objection,
that is.

GREGERS.

None in the world! How can I object to a step-
mother who is playing Blind Man's Buff at the
present moment with the Norwegian nobility? I am
not so overstrained as all that. But really I cannot
allow my old friend Hialmar, with his great, con-
fiding, childlike mind, to remain in contented ignorance of Gina's past. No, I see my mission in life at
last! I shall take my hat, and inform him that his
home is built upon a lie. He will be *so* much
obliged to me!   *[Takes his hat, and goes out.*

OLD WERLE.

Ha!—I am a wealthy merchant, of dubious morals,
and I am about to marry my housekeeper, who is on
intimate terms with the Norwegian aristocracy. I
have a son who loathes me, and who is either an
Ibsenian satire on the Master's own ideals, or else an
utterly impossible prig—I don't know or care which.
Altogether, I flatter myself my household affords an
accurate and realistic picture of Scandinavian Society!

Curtain.

ACT SECOND

HIALMAR EKDAL'S *Photographic Studio. Cameras, neck-rests, and other instruments of torture lying about.* GINA EKDAL *and* HEDWIG, *her daughter, aged* 14, *and wearing spectacles, discovered sitting up for* HIALMAR.

HEDVIG.

Grandpapa is in his room with a bottle of brandy and a jug of hot water, doing some fresh copying work. Father is in society, dining out. He promised he would bring me home something nice!

HIALMAR.

[*Coming in, in evening dress.*] And he has not forgotten his promise, my child. Behold! [*He *presents her with the menu card;* HEDVIG *gulps down her tears;* HIALMAR *notices her disappointment, with annoyance.*] And this all the gratitude I get! After dining out and coming home in a dress-coat and boots, which are disgracefully tight! Well well, just to show you how hurt I am, I won't have any *beer* now! What a selfish brute I am! [*Relenting.*] You may bring me just a little drop. [*He bursts into tears.*] I will play you a plaintive Bohemian dance on my flute. [*He does.*] No beer at such a sacred moment as this! [*He drinks.*] Ha, this is real domestic bliss!

[GREGERS WERLE *comes in, in a countrified suit.*

GREGERS.

I have left my father's home—dinner-party and all —for ever. I am coming to lodge with you.

HIALMAR.

[*Still melancholy.*] Have some bread and butter. You won't?—then I *will.* I want it, after your father's lavish hospitality. [HEDVIG *goes to fetch bread and butter.*] My daughter—a poor short-sighted little thing—but mine own.

GREGERS.

My father has had to take to strong glasses, too—he can hardly see after dinner. [*To* Old EKDAL, *who stumbles in very drunk.*] How can you, Lieutenant Ekdal, who were such a keen sportsman once, live in this poky little hole?

OLD EKDAL.

I am a sportsman still. The only difference is that once I shot bears in a forest, and now I pot tame rabbits in a garret. Quite as amusing—and safer. [*He goes to sleep on a sofa.*

HIALMAR.

[*With pride.*] It is quite true. You shall see.

[*He pushes back sliding doors, and reveals a garret full of rabbits and poultry—moonlight effect.* HEDVIG *returns with bread and butter.*

HEDVIG.

[*To* GREGERS.] If you stand just there, you get the best view of our Wild Duck. We are very proud of her, because she gives the play its title, you know, and has to be brought into the dialogue a good deal. Your father peppered her out shooting, and we saved her life.

HIALMAR.

Yes, Gregers, our estate is not large—but still we preserve, you see. And my poor old father and I sometimes get a day's gunning in the garret. He shoots with a pistol, which my illiterate wife here *will* call a " pigstol." He once, when he got into trouble, pointed it at himself. But the descendant of two lieutenant-colonels who had never quailed before living rabbit yet, faltered then. He *didn't* shoot. Then I put it to my own head. But at the decisive moment, I won the victory over myself. I remained in life. Now we only shoot rabbits and fowls with it. After all I am very happy and contented as I am. [*He eats some bread and butter.*

GREGERS.

But you ought *not* to be. You have a good deal of the Wild Duck about you. So have your wife and daughter. You are living in marsh vapours. To-morrow I will take you out for a walk and explain what I mean. It is my mission in life. Good night!

[*He goes out.*

GINA AND HEDWIG.

What *was* the gentleman talking about, father?

HIALMAR.

[*Eating bread and butter.*] He has been dining, you know. No matter—what *we* have to do now, is to put my disreputable old whitehaired pariah of a parent to bed.

[*He and* GINA *lift* Old ECCLES—*we mean* Old EKDAL—*up by the legs and arms, and take him off to bed as the Curtain falls.*

ACT THREE

HIALMAR's *Studio. A photograph has just been taken.*
GINA *and* HEDVIG *are tidying up.*

GINA.

[*Apologetically.*] There *should* have been a luncheon-party in this act, with Dr. Relling and Mölvik, who would have been in a state of comic "chippiness," after his excesses overnight.   But, as it hadn't much to do with such plot as there is, we cut it out.   It came cheaper.   Here comes your father back from his walk with that lunatic, young Werle—you had better go and play with the Wild Duck.

[HEDVIG *goes.*

HIALMAR.

[*Coming in.*] I have been for a walk with Gregers; he meant well—but it was tiring. Gina, he has told me that, fifteen years ago, before I married you, you were rather a Wild Duck, so to speak. [*Severely.*] Why haven't you been writhing in penitence and remorse all these years, eh?

GINA.

[*Sensibly.*] Why? Because I have had other things to do. *You* wouldn't take any photographs, so I *had* to.

HIALMAR.

All the same—it was a swamp of deceit. And where am I to find elasticity of spirit to bring out my grand invention now? I used to shut myself up in the parlour, and ponder and cry, when I thought that the effort of inventing anything would sap my vitality. [*Pathetically.*] I *did* want to leave you an inventor's widow; but I never shall now, particularly

as I haven't made up my mind what to invent yet.
Yes, it's all over. Rabbits are trash, and even
poultry palls. And I'll wring that cursed Wild
Duck's neck !

GREGERS.

[*Coming in beaming.*] Well, so you've got it over.
Wasn't it soothing and ennobling, eh ? and *ain't* you
both obliged to me ?

GINA.

No ; it's my opinion you'd better have minded
your own business.   [*Weeps.*

GREGERS.

[*In great surprise.*] Bless me ! Pardon my Norwegian *naïveté*, but this ought really to be quite a
new starting-point. Why, I confidently expected to
have found you both beaming !—Mrs. Ekdal, being
so illiterate, may take some little time to see it—but
you, Hialmar, with your deep mind, surely *you* feel
a new consecration, eh ?

HIALMAR.

[*Dubiously.*] Oh—er—yes. I suppose so—in a sort of way. [HEDVIG *runs in, overjoyed.*

HEDVIG.

Father, only see what Mrs. Sörby has given me for a birthday present—a beautiful deed of gift!

[*Shows it.*

HIALMAR.

[*Eluding her.*] Ha! Mrs. Sörby, the family house-keeper. ~~My father's~~ *Old Werle's* sight failing! Hedvig in goggles! What vistas of heredity these astonishing coincidences open up! *I* am not short-sighted, at all events, and I see it all—all! *This* is my answer. [*He takes the deed, and tears it across.*] Now I have nothing more to do in this house. [*Puts on over-coat.*] My home has fallen in ruins about me. [*Bursts into tears.*] My hat!

GREGERS.

Oh, but you *mustn't* go. You must be all three

together, to attain the true frame of mind for self-sacrificing forgiveness, you know!

HIALMAR.

Self-sacrificing forgiveness be blowed!

[*He tears himself away, and goes out.*

HEDVIG.

[*With despairing eyes.*] Oh, he said it might be blowed! Now he'll *never* come home any more!

GREGERS.

Shall I tell you how to regain your father's confidence, and bring him home surely? Sacrifice the Wild Duck.

HEDVIG.

Do you think that will do any good?

GREGERS.

You just *try* it!

Curtain.

ACT FOURTH

Same Scene. GREGERS *enters, and finds* GINA *retouching photographs.*

GREGERS.

[*Pleasantly.*] Hialmar not come in yet, after last night, I suppose?

GINA.

Not he! He's been out on the loose all night with Relling and Mölvik. Now he's snoring on their sofa.

GREGERS.

[*Disappointed.*] Dear!—dear!—when he ought to be yearning to wrestle in solitude and self-examination!

K

GINA.

[*Rudely.*] Self-examine your grandmother!

[*She goes out;* HEDVIG *comes in.*

GREGERS.

[*To* HEDVIG.] Ah, I see you haven't found courage to settle the Wild Duck yet!

HEDVIG.

No—it seemed such a delightful idea at first. Now it strikes me as a trifle—well, *Ibsenish.*

GREGERS.

[*Reprovingly.*] I *thought* you hadn't grown up quite unharmed in this house! But if you really had the true, joyous spirit of self-sacrifice, you'd have a shot at that Wild Duck, if you died for it!

HEDVIG.

[*Slowly.*] I see; you mean that my constitution's changing, and I ought to behave as such?

GREGERS.

Exactly, I'm what Americans would term a " crank "
—but *I* believe in you, Hedvig.

> [HEDVIG *takes down the pistol from the*
> *mantelpiece, and goes into the garret with*
> *flashing eyes;* GINA *comes in.*

HIALMAR.

[*Looking in at door with hesitation; he is unwashed*
and dishevelled.] Has anybody happened to see my
hat ?

GINA.

Gracious, what a sight you are !   Sit done and have
some breakfast, do.   [*She brings it.*

HIALMAR.

[*Indignantly.*] What ! touch food under *this* roof ?
Never !   [*Helps himself to bread-and-butter and coffee.*]
Go and pack up my scientific uncut books, my manu-
scripts, and all the best rabbits, in my portmanteau.
I am going away for ever.   On second thoughts, I

shall stay in the spare room for another day or two—
it won't be the same as living with you!

        [He takes some salt meat.

GREGERS.

Must you go? Just when you've got nice firm
ground to build upon—thanks to me! Then there's
your great invention, too.

HIALMAR.

Everything's invented already. And I only cared
about my invention because, although it doesn't exist
yet, I thought Hedvig believed in it, with all the
strength of her sweet little shortsighted eyes! But
now I don't believe in Hedvig!

        [He pours himself out another cup of coffee.

GREGERS.

[*Earnestly.*] But, Hialmar, if I can prove to you
that she is ready to sacrifice her cherished Wild
Duck? See!

        [He pushes back sliding-door, and discovers
        HEDVIG *aiming at the* Wild Duck *with the*
        butt-end of the pistol. Tableau.

GINA.

[*Excitedly.*] But don't you *see?* It's the pigstol—
that fatal Norwegian weapon which, in Ibsenian
dramas, *never* shoots straight! And she has got it by
the wrong end too. She will shoot herself!

GREGERS.

[*Quietly.*] She will! Let the child make amends.
It will be a most realistic and impressive finale!

GINA.

No, no—put down the pigstol, Hedvig. Do you
hear, child?

HEDVIG.

[*Still aiming.*] I hear—but I shan't unless father
tells me to.

GREGERS.

Hialmar, show the great soul I always *said* you had.
This sorrow will set free what is noble in you. Don't
spoil a fine situation. Be a man! Let the child
shoot herself!

HIALMAR.

[*Irresolutely.*] Well, really, I don't know. There's a good deal in what Gregers says. H'm!

GINA.

A good deal of tomfool rubbish! I'm illiterate, I know. I've been a Wild Duck in my time, and I waddle. But for all that, I'm the only person in the play with a grain of common-sense. And I'm sure—whatever Mr. Ibsen or Gregers choose to say—that a screaming burlesque like this ought *not* to end like a tragedy—even in this queer Norway of ours! And it shan't, either! Tell the child to put that nasty pigstol down, and come away—do!

HIALMAR.

[*Yielding.*] Ah, well, I am a farcical character myself, after all. Don't touch a hair of that duck's head, Hedvig. Come to my arms and all shall be forgiven!

> [HEDVIG *throws down the pistol—which goes*
> *off and kills a rabbit—and rushes into her*

" Put that nasty pigstol down ! "

father's arms. Old EKDAL *comes out of a corner with a fowl on each shoulder, and bursts into tears. Affecting family picture.*

GREGERS.

[*Annoyed.*] It's all very pretty, I dare say—but it's not Ibsen! My real mission is to be the thirteenth at table. I don't know what I mean—but I fly to fulfil it! [*He goes.*

HIALMAR.

And now we've got rid of *him*, Hedvig, fetch me the deed of gift I tore up, and a slip of paper, and a penny bottle of gum, and we'll soon make a valid instrument of it again.

[*He pastes the torn deed together as the Curtain slowly descends.*

PILL-DOCTOR HERDAL

PILL-DOCTOR HERDAL

[PREFATORY NOTE.—The original title—*Mester-Pjil-drögster Herdal*—would sound a trifle too uncouth to the Philistine ear. and is therefore modified as above, although the term "drögster," strictly speaking, denotes a practitioner who has not received a regular diploma].

ACT FIRST

An elegantly furnished drawing-room at Dr. HERDAL'S.
*In front, on the left, a console-table, on which is a
large round bottle full of coloured water. On the
right a store, with a banner-screen made out of a
richly-embroidered chest-protector. On the store, a
stethoscope and a small galvanic battery. In one
corner, a hat and umbrella stand : in another, a*

desk, at which stands SENNA BLAKDRAF, *making out the quarterly accounts. Through a glass-door at the back is seen the Dispensary, where* RŪBUB KALOMEL *is seated, occupied in rolling a pill. Both go on working in perfect silence for four minutes and a half.*

DR. HAUSTUS HERDAL.

[*Enters through hall-door; he is elderly, with a plain sensible countenance, but slightly weak hair and expression.*] Come here Miss Blakdraf. [*Hangs up hat, and throws his mackintosh on a divan.*] Have you made out all those bills yet?

[Looks sternly at her.

SENNA.

[*In a low hesitating voice.*] Almost. I have charged each patient with three attendances daily. Even when you only dropped in for a cup of tea and a chat. [*Passionately.*] I felt I must—I must!

Dr. Herdal.

[*Alters his tone, clasps her head in his hands, and whispers.*] I wish you could make out the bills for me, *always.*

Senna.

[*In nervous exaltation.*] How lovely that would be! Oh, you are so unspeakably good to me! It is too enthralling to be here!

[*Sinks down and embraces his knees.*

Dr. Herdal.

So I've understood. [*With suppressed irritation.*] For goodness' sake, let go my legs! I do *wish* you wouldn't be so confoundedly neurotic!

Rubub.

[*Has risen, and comes in through glass-door, breathing with difficulty; he is a prematurely bald young man of fifty-five, with a harelip, and squints slightly.*] I beg pardon, Dr. Herdal, I see I interrupt you. [*As* SENNA *rises.*] I have just completed this pill. Have you looked at it ?

> [*He offers it for inspection, diffidently.*

DR. HERDAL.

[*Evasively.*] It appears to be a pill of the usual dimensions.

RÜBUB.

[*Cast down.*] All these years you have never given me one encouraging word ! *Can't* you praise my pill ?

DR. HERDAL.

[*Struggles with himself.*] I—I cannot. You should not attempt to compound pills on your own account.

RÜBUB.

[*Breathing laboriously.*] And yet there was a time when *you*, too——

DR. HERDAL.

[*Complacently.*] Yes, it was certainly a pill that came as a lucky stepping-stone—but not a pill like that !

"For goodness' sake, let go my legs!"

L

Rubub.

[*Vehemently.*] Listen! Is that your last word? *Is* my aged mother to pass out of this world without ever knowing whether I am competent to construct an effective pill or not?

Dr. Herdal.

[*As if in desperation.*] You had better try it upon your mother—it will enable her to form an opinion. Only mind—I will not be responsible for the result.

Rubub.

I understand. Exactly as you tried *your* pill, all those years ago, upon Dr. Ryval.

[*He bows and goes out.*

Dr. Herdal.

[*Uneasily.*] He said that so strangely, Senna. But tell me now—when are you going to marry him?

SENNA.

[*Starts—half glancing up at him.*] I—I don't
know. This year—next year—now—*never!* I cannot marry him ... I cannot—I *cannot*—it is so
utterly impossible to leave you!

DR. HERDAL.

Yes, I can understand *that.* But, my poor Senna,
hadn't you better take a little walk?

SENNA.

[*Clasps her hands gratefully.*] How sweet and
thoughtful you are to me! I *will* take a walk.

DR. HERDAL.

[*With a suppressed smile.*] Do! And—h'm!—you
needn't trouble to come back. I have advertised for
a male book-keeper—they are less emotional. Good-
night, my little Senna!

SENNA.

[*Softly and quiveringly.*] Good-night, Dr. Herdal!

[*Staggers out of hall-door, blowing kisses.*

MRS. HERDAL.

[*Enters through the window, plaintively.*] Quite an acquisition for you, Haustus, this Miss Blakdraf!

DR. HERDAL.

She's—h'm—extremely civil and obliging. But I am parting with her, Aline—mainly on *your* account.

MRS. HERDAL.

[*Evades him.*] Was it on my account, indeed, Haustus? You have parted with so many young persons on my account—so you tell me!

DR. HERDAL.

[*Depressed.*] Oh, but this is hopeless! When I have tried so hard to bring a ray of sunlight into your desolate life! I must give Rübub Kalomel notice too—his pill is really too preposterous!

MRS. HERDAL.

[*Feels gropingly for a chair, and sits down on the floor.*] Him, *too!* Ah, Haustus, you will never make my home a real home for me. My poor first husband, Halvard Solness, tried—and *he* couldn't! When one has had such misfortunes as I have—all the family portraits burnt, and the silk dresses, too, and a pair of twins, and nine lovely dolls.

[*Chokes with tears.*

DR. HERDAL.

[*As if to lead her away from the subject.*] Yes, yes, yes, that must have been a heavy blow for you, my poor Aline. I can understand that your spirits can never be really high again. And then for poor Master Builder Solness to be so taken up with that Miss Wangel as he was—that, too, was so wretched for you. To see him topple off the tower, as he did that day ten years ago——

Mrs. Herdal.

Yes, that too, Haustus. But I did not mind it so much—it all seemed so perfectly natural in both of them.

Dr. Herdal.

Natural! For a girl of twenty three to taunt a middle-aged architect, whom she knew to be constitutionally liable to giddiness, never to let him have any peace till he had climbed a spire as dizzy as himself—and all for the fun of seeing him fall off—how in the world—— !

Mrs. Herdal.

[*Laying the table for supper with dried fish and punch.*] The younger generation have a keener sense of humour than we elder ones, Haustus, and perhaps after all, she was only a perplexing sort of allegory.

Dr. Herdal.

Yes, that would explain her to some extent, no doubt. ·But how *he* could be such an old fool !

MRS. HERDAL.

That Miss Wangel was a strangely fascinating type of girl. Why, even I myself——

DR. HERDAL.

[*Sits down and takes some fish.*] Fascinating? Well, goodness knows, I couldn't see *that* at all. [*Seriously.*] Has it never struck you, Aline, that elderly Norwegians are so deucedly impressionable—mere bundles of overstrained nerves, hypersensitive ganglia. Except, of course, the Medical Profession.

MRS. HERDAL.

Yes, of course; those in that profession are not so inclined to gangle. And when one has succeeded by such a stroke of luck as you have——

DR. HERDAL.

[*Drinks a glass of punch.*] You're right enough there. If I had not been called in to prescribe for Dr. Ryval, who used to have the leading practice here, I should never have stepped so wonderfully into his shoes as I did. [*Changes to a tone of quiet chuck-ling merriment.*] Let me tell you a funny story, Aline; it sounds a ludicrous thing—but all my good fortune here was based upon a simple little pill. For if Dr. Ryval had never taken it——

Mrs. Herdal.

[*Anxiously.*] Then you *do* think it was the pill that caused him to—— ?

Dr. Herdal.

On the contrary; I am perfectly sure the pill had nothing whatever to do with it—the inquest made it quite clear that it was really the liniment. But don't you see, Aline, what tortures me night and day is the thought that it *might* unconsciously have been the pill which—— Never to be free from *that !* To have such a thought gnawing and burning always—always, like a moral mustard plaster !

[*He takes more punch.*

Mrs. Herdal.

Yes; I suppose there is a poultice of that sort burning on every breast—and we must never take it off either—it is our simple duty to keep it on. I too, Haustus, am haunted by a fancy that if this Miss Wangel were to ring at our bell now——

Dr. Herdal.

After she has been lost sight of for ten years? She is safe enough in some sanatorium, depend upon it. And what if she *did* come? Do you think, my dear good woman, that I—a sensible clear-headed general practitioner, who have found out all I know for myself—would let her play the deuce with me as she did with poor Halvard? No, general practitioners don't *do* such things—even in Norway!

Mrs. Herdal.

Don't they indeed, Haustus? [*The surgery-bell rings loudly.*] Did you hear *that?* There she is! I will go and put on my best cap. It is my duty to show her *that* small attention.

Dr. Herdal.

[*Laughing nervously.*] Why, what on earth !——
It's the night-bell. It is most probably the new
book-keeper! [Mrs. Herdal *goes out;* Dr. Herdal
rises with difficulty, and opens the door.] Goodness
gracious !—it *is* that girl, after all !

[Hilda Wangel *enters through the dispensary door.
She wears a divided skirt, thick boots, and a Tam
o' Shanter with an eagle's wing in it. Somewhat
freckled. Carries a green tin cylinder slung round her,
and a rug in a strap. Goes straight up to* Herdal,
her eyes sparkling with happiness.] How are you?
I've run you down, you see ! The ten years are up.
Isn't it scrumptiously thrilling, to see me like this?

Dr. Herdal.

[*Politely retreating.*] It is—very much so—but still
I don't in the least understand——

HILDA.

[*Measures him with a glance.*] Oh, you *will*. I have come to be of use to you. I've no luggage, and no money. Not that *that* makes any difference. I never *have*. And I've been allured and attracted here. You surely know how these things come about?   [*Throws her arms round him.*

DR. HERDAL.

What the deuce! Miss Wangel, you *mustn't*. I'm a married man! There's my wife!

MRS. HERDAL *enters.*

HILDA.

As if *that* mattered—it's only dear, sweet Mrs. Solness. *She* doesn't mind—*do* you, dear Mrs. Solness?

MRS. HERDAL.

It does not seem to be of much *use* minding, Miss Wangel. I presume you have come to stay?

Hilda.

[*In amused surprise.*] Why, of course—what else should I come for? I *always* come to stay, until— h'm! [*Nods slowly, and sits down at table.*

Dr. Herdal.

[*Involuntarily.*] She's drinking my punch! If she thinks I'm going to stand this sort of thing, she's mistaken. I'll soon show her a pill-doctor is a very different kind of person from a mere Master Builder!

> [Hilda *finishes the punch with an indefinable expression in her eyes, and* Dr. Herdal *looks on gloomily as the Curtain falls.*

ACT SECOND

Dr. HERDAL's *drawing-room and dispensary, as before. It is early in the day.* DR. HERDAL *sits by the little table, taking his own temperature with a clinical thermometer. By the door stands the* NEW BOOK-KEEPER; *he wears blue spectacles and a discoloured white tie, and seems slightly nervous.*

DR. HERDAL.

Well, now you understand what is necessary. My late book-keeper, Miss Blakdraf, used to keep my accounts very cleverly—she charged every visit twice over.

THE NEW BOOK-KEEPER.

I am familiar with book-keeping by double entry. I was once employed at a bank.

DR. HERDAL.

I am discharging my assistant, too; he was always trying to push me out with his pills. Perhaps you will be able to dispense?

THE NEW BOOK-KEEPER.

[*Modestly.*] With an additional salary, I should be able to do that too.

DR. HERDAL.

Capital! You *shall* dispense with an additional salary. Go into the dispensary, and see what you can make of it. You may mistake a few drugs at first —but everything must have a beginning.

> [*As the* NEW BOOK-KEEPER *retires,* MRS. HERDAL *enters in a hat and cloak with a watering-pot, noiselessly.*

Mrs. Herdal.

Miss Wangel got up early, before breakfast, and went for a walk. She is so wonderfully vivacious!

Dr. Herdal.

So I should say. But tell me, Aline, is she *really* going to stay with us here?   [*Nervously.*

Mrs. Herdal.

[*Looks at him.*] So she tells me. And, as she has brought nothing with her except a tooth-brush and a powder-puff, I am going into the town to get her a few articles. We *must* make her feel at home.

Dr. Herdal.

[*Breaking out.*] I *will* make her not only *feel* but *be* at home, wherever that is, this very day! I will *not* have a perambulating Allegory without a portmanteau here on an indefinite visit. I say, she shall go—do you hear, Aline? Miss Wangel will go!

[*Raps with his fist on table.*

Mrs. Herdal.

[*Quietly.*] If you say so, Haustus, no doubt she will *have* to go. But you must tell her so yourself.

> [*Puts the watering-pot on the console table,
> and goes out, as* Hilda *enters, sparkling
> with pleasure.*

Hilda.

[*Goes up straight to him.*] Good morning, Dr. Herdal. I have just seen a pig killed. It was *ripping*—I mean, gloriously thrilling! And your wife has taken a tremendous fancy to me. Fancy *that!*

Dr. Herdal.

[*Gloomily.*] It *is* eccentric certainly. But my poor dear wife was always a little——

Hilda.

[*Nods her head slowly several times.*] So *you* have noticed that too? I have had a long talk with her. She can't get over your discharging Mr. Kalomel—he is the only man who ever *really* understood her.

M

Dr. Herdal.

If I could only pay her off a little bit of the huge, immeasurable debt I owe her—but I can't!

Hilda.

[*Looks hard at him.*] Can't *I* help you? I helped Ragnar Brovik. Didn't you know I stayed with him and poor little Kaia—after that accident to my Master Builder? I did. I made Ragnar build me the loveliest castle in the air—lovelier, even, than poor Mr. Solness's would have been—and we stood together on the very top. The steps were rather too much for Kaia. Besides, there was no room for her on top. And he put towering spires on all his semi-detached villas. Only, somehow, they didn't let. Then the castle in the air tumbled down, and Ragnar went into liquidation, and I continued my walking-tour.

Dr. Herdal.

[*Interested against his will.*] And where did you go after *that*, may I ask, Miss Wangel?

HILDA.

Oh, ever so far north. There I met Mr. and Mrs. Tesman—the second Mrs. Tesman—she who was Mrs. Elvsted, with the irritating hair, you know. They were on their honeymoon, and had just decided that it was impossible to reconstruct poor Mr. Lövborg's great book out of Mrs. Elvsted's rough notes. But I insisted on George's attempting the impossible—with Me. And what *do* you think Mrs. Tesman wears in her hair *now ?*

DR. HERDAL.

Why, really I could not say. Vine-leaves, perhaps.

HILDA.

Wrong—*straws !* Poor Tesman *didn't* fancy that— so he shot himself, *un*-beautifully, through his ticket-pocket. And I went on and took Rosmersholm for the summer. There had been misfortune in the house, so it was to let. Dear good old Rector Kroll acted as my reference; his wife and children had no

sympathy with his views, so I used to see him every
day. And I persuaded him, too, to attempt the
impossible—he had never ridden anything but a
rocking-horse in his life, but I made him promise to
mount the White Horse of Rosmersholm. He
didn't get over *that.* They found his body, a fortnight
afterwards, in the mill-dam. Thrilling!

DR. HERDAL.

[*Shakes his finger at her.*] What a girl you are, Miss
Wangel! But you mustn't play these games *here,* you
know.

HILDA.

[*Laughs to herself.*] Of course not. But I suppose
I *am* a strange sort of bird.

DR. HERDAL.

You are like a strong tonic. When I look at you
I seem to be regarding an effervescing saline draught.
Still, I really must decline to take you.

HILDA.

[*A little sulky.*] That is not how you spoke ten years ago, up at the mountain station, when you were such a flirt!

DR. HERDAL.

Was I a flirt? Deuce take me if I remember. But I am not like that *now*.

HILDA.

Then you have really forgotten how you sat next to me at the *table d'hôte*, and made pills and swallowed them, and were so splendid and buoyant and free that all the old women who knitted left next day?

DR. HERDAL.

What a memory you have for trifles, Miss Wangel; it's quite wonderful!

HILDA.

Trifles! There was no trifling on *your* part. When you promised to come back in ten years, like a troll, and fetch me!

DR. HERDAL.

Did I say all that? It *must* have been *after table d'hôte!*

HILDA.

It was. I was a mere chit then—only twenty-three; but *I* remember. And now *I* have come for *you.*

DR. HERDAL.

Dear, dear! But there is nothing of the troll about me now I have married Mrs. Solness.

HILDA.

[*Looking sharply at him.*] Yes, I remember you were always dropping in to tea in those days.

Dr. Herdal.

[*Seems hurt.*] Every visit was duly put down in the ledger and charged for—as poor little Senna will tell you.

Hilda.

Little Senna? Oh, Dr. Herdal, I believe there is a bit of the troll left in you still!

Dr. Herdal.

[*Laughs a little.*] No, no; my conscience is perfectly robust—always was.

Hilda.

Are you quite *quite* sure that, when you went indoors with dear Mrs. Solness that afternoon, and left me alone with my Master Builder, you did not foresee—perhaps wish—intend, even a little, that—— H'm?

Dr. Herdal.

That you would talk the poor man into clambering up that tower? You want to drag *Me* into that business now!

HILDA.

[*Teasingly.*] Yes, I certainly think that then you went on exactly like a troll.

DR. HERDAL.

[*With uncontrollable emotion.*] Hilda, there is not a corner of me safe from you! Yes, I see now that *must* have been the way of it. Then I *was* a troll in that, too! But isn't it terrible the price I have had to pay for it? To have a wife who—— No, I shall never roll a pill again—never, never!

HILDA.

[*Lays her head on the stove, and answers as if half asleep.*] No more pills? Poor Doctor Herdal!

DR. HERDAL.

[*Bitterly.*] No—nothing but cosy commonplace grey powders for a whole troop of children.

HILDA.

[*Lively again.*] Not *grey* powders! [*Quite seriously.*] I will tell you what you shall make next. Beautiful

" Beautiful rainbow-coloured powders that will give
one a real grip on the world!"

rainbow-coloured powders that will give one a real
grip on the world. Powders to make every one free
and buoyant, and ready to grasp at one's own happiness, to *dare* what one *would*. I will have you make
them. I will—I *will!*

Dr. Herdal.

H'm! I am not quite sure that I clearly understand. And then the ingredients—— ?

Hilda.

What stupid people all of you pill-doctors are, to be
sure! Why, they will be *poisons*, of course!

Dr. Herdal.

Poisons? Why in the world should they be *that?*

Hilda.

[*Without answering him.*] All the thrillingest,
deadliest poisons—it is only such things that are
wholesome, nowadays.

DR. HERDAL.

[*As if caught by her enthusiasm.*] And I could colour them, too, by exposing them to rays cast through a prism. Oh, Hilda, how I have needed you all these years! For, you see, with *her* it was impossible to discuss such things.   [*Embraces her.*

MRS. HERDAL.

[*Enters noiselessly through hall-door.*] I suppose, Haustus, you are persuading Miss Wangel to start by the afternoon steamer? I have bought her a pair of curling-tongs, and a packet of hair-pins. The larger parcels are coming on presently.

DR. HERDAL.

[*Uneasily.*] H'm! Hilda—Miss Wangel I *should* say—is kindly going to stay on a little longer, to assist me in some scientific experiments. You wouldn't understand them if I told you.

Mrs. Herdal.

Shouldn't I, Haustus? I daresay not.

[*The* New Book-keeper *looks through the glass door of dispensary.*]

Hilda.

[*Starts violently and points—then in a whisper.*] Who is *that?*

Dr. Herdal.

Only the new Book-keeper and Assistant—a very intelligent person.

Hilda.

[*Looks straight in front of her with a far-away expression, and whispers to herself.*] I thought at first it was . . . . But no—*that* would be *too* frightfully thrilling!

Dr. Herdal.

[*To himself.*] I'm turning into a regular old troll

now—but I can't help myself.   After all, I am only an elderly Norwegian.   We are *made* like that . . . . Rainbow powders—*real* rainbow powders!   With Hilda! . . . . Oh, to have the joy of life once more!

[*Takes his temperature again as Curtain falls.*

ACT THIRD

[*On the right, a smart verandah, attached to* Dr. Herdal's *dwelling-house, and communicating with the drawing-room and dispensary by glass doors. On the left a tumble-down rockery, with a headless plaster Mercury. In front, a lawn, with a large silvered glass globe on a stand. Chairs and tables. All the furniture is of galvanised iron. A sunset is seen going on among the trees.*

Dr. Herdal.

[*Comes out of dispensary-door cautiously, and whispers.*] Hilda, are you in there?

[*Taps with fingers on drawing-room door.*

HILDA.

[*Comes out with a half-teasing smile.*] Well—and how is the rainbow-powder getting on, Dr. Herdal?

DR. HERDAL.

[*With enthusiasm.*] It is getting on simply splendidly. I sent the new assistant out to take a little walk, so that he should not be in the way. There is arsenic in the powder, Hilda, and digitalis too, and strychnine, and the best beetle-killer!

HILDA.

[*With happy, wondering eyes.*] *Lots* of beetle-killer   And you will give some of it to *her*, to make her free and buoyant. I think one really *has* the right—when people happen to stand in the way—— !

DR. HERDAL.

Yes, you may well say so, Hilda. Still—[*dubiously*] —it *does* occur to me that such doings may perhaps be misunderstood—by the narrow-minded and conventional.   [*They go on the lawn, and sit down.*

HILDA.

[*With an outburst.*] Oh, that all seems to me so foolish—so irrelevant! As if the whole thing wasn't intended as an allegory!

DR. HERDAL.

[*Relieved.*] Ah, so long as it is merely *allegorical*, of course—— But what is it an allegory *of*, Hilda?

HILDA.

[*Reflects in vain.*] How can you sit there and ask such questions? I suppose I am a symbol—of some sort.

DR. HERDAL.

[*As a thought flashes upon him.*] A cymbal? That would certainly account for your bra—— Then, am *I* a cymbal too, Hilda?

HILDA.

Why yes—what else? You represent the artist-worker, or the elder generation, or the pursuit of

N

the ideal, or a bilious conscience—or something or other. *You're* all right!

Dr. Herdal.

[*Shakes his head.*] Am I? But I don't quite see —— Well, well, cymbals are meant to clash a little. And I see plainly now that I ought to prescribe this powder for as many as possible. Isn't it terrible, Hilda, that so many poor souls never really die their own deaths—pass out of the world without even the formality of an inquest? As the district Coroner, I feel strongly on the subject.

Hilda.

And, when the Coroner has finished sitting on all the bodies, perhaps—but I shan't tell you now. [*Speaks as if to a child.*] There, run away and finish making the rainbow-powder, do!

Dr. Herdal.

[*Skips up into the dispensary.*] I will—I will! Oh, I do feel such a troll—such a light-haired, light-headed old devil!

RUBUB.

[*Enters garden-gate.*] I have had my dismissal—but I'm not going without saying good-bye to Mrs. Herdal.

HILDA.

Dr. Herdal would disapprove—you really must not, Mr. Kalomel. And, besides, Mrs. Herdal is not at home. She is in the town buying me a reel of cotton. *Dr.* Herdal is in. He is making real rainbow powders for regenerating everybody all round. Won't *that* be fun?

RUBUB.

Making powders? Ha! ha! But you will see he won't *take* one himself. It is quite notorious to us younger men that he simply daren't do it.

HILDA.

[*With a little snort of contempt.*] Oh, I daresay—that's so likely! [*Defiantly.*] I know he *can*, though. I've *seen* him!

Rubub.

There is a tradition that he once—but not now
—he knows better. I think you said Mrs. Herdal
was in the town? I will go and look for her. I
understand her so well.   [*Goes out by gate.*

Hilda.

[*Calls.*] Dr. Herdal! Come out this minute. I
want you—awfully!

Dr. Herdal.

[*Puts his head out.*] Just when I am making such
wonderful progress with the powder. [*Comes down
and leans on a table.*] Have you hit upon some way
of giving it to Aline? I thought if you were to put
it in her arrowroot—— ?

Hilda.

No, thanks. I won't have that now. I have just
recollected that it is a rule of mine never to injure
anybody I have once been formally introduced to.

Strangers don't count. No, poor Mrs. Herdal
mustn't take that powder !

DR. HERDAL.

[*Disappointed.*] Then is nothing to come of making
rainbow powders, after all, Hilda ?

HILDA.

[*Looks hard at him.*] People say you are afraid to
take your own physic. Is that true ?

DR. HERDAL.

Yes, I am. [*After a pause—with candour.*] I find
it invariably disagrees with me.

HILDA.

[*With a half-dubious smile.*] I think I can understand *that*. But you did *once*. You swallowed your
own pills that day at the *table d'hôte*, ten years ago.
And I heard a harp in the air, too !

DR. HERDAL.

[*Open-mouthed.*] I don't think that *could* have been
me. I don't play any instrument. And that was

quite a special thing, too. It's not every day I can
do it. Those were only *bread* pills, Hilda.

HILDA.

[*With flashing eyes.*] But you rolled them, you
took them. And I want to see you stand once more
free and high and great, swallowing your own preparations. [*Passionately.*] I *will* have you do it!
[*Imploringly.*] Just once more, Dr. Herdal!

DR. HERDAL.

If I did, Hilda, my medical knowledge, slight as it
is, leads me to the conclusion that I should in all
probability burst.

HILDA.

[*Looks deeply into his eyes.*] So long as you burst
beautifully! But no doubt that Miss Blakdraf——

DR. HERDAL.

You must believe in me utterly and entirely. I
will do anything—*anything*, Hilda, to provide you

with agreeable entertainment. I *will* swallow my
own powder! [*To himself, as he goes gravely up
to dispensary.*] If only the drugs are sufficiently
adulterated!

> [*Goes in; as he does so, the* NEW ASSISTANT
> *enters the garden in blue spectacles, unseen
> by* HILDA, *and follows him, leaving open
> the glass door.*

SENNA.

[*Comes wildly out of drawing-room.*] Where is dear
Dr. Herdal? Oh, Miss Wangel, he has discharged
me—but I can't—I simply *can't* live away from that
lovely ledger.

HILDA.

[*Jubilantly.*] At this moment Dr. Herbal is in the
dispensary, taking one of his own powders.

SENNA.

[*Despairingly.*] But—but it is utterly impossible!
Miss Wangel, you have such a firm hold of him—*don't*
let him do that!

HILDA.

I have already done all I can.

[RÜBUB *appears, talking confidentially with*
MRS. HERDAL, *at gate.*

SENNA.

Oh, Mrs. Herdal, Rübub! The Pill-Doctor is
going to take one of his own preparations. Save him
—quick !

RÜBUB.

[*With cold politeness.*] I am sorry to hear it—for
his sake. But it would be quite contrary to professional etiquette to prevent him.

MRS. HERDAL.

And I never interfere with my husband's proceedings. I know *my* duty, Miss Blakdraf, if *others*
don't !

HILDA.

[*Exulting with great intensity.*] At last! Now I
see him in there, great and free again, mixing the

powder in a spoon—with jam! . . . . Now he raises
the spoon. Higher—higher still! [*A gulp is audible
from within.*] There, didn't you hear a harp in the
air? [*Quietly.*] 1 can't see the spoon any more.
But there is one he is striving with, in blue spectacles!

The New Assistant's Voice.

[*Within.*] The Pill-Doctor Herdal has taken his own
powder!

Hilda.

[*As if petrified.*] That voice! *Where* have 1 heard
it before? No matter—he has got the powder down!
[*Waves a shawl in the air, and shrieks with wild
jubilation.*] It's too awfully thrilling! My—*my* Pill-
Doctor!

The New Assistant.

[*Comes out on verandah.*] I am happy to inform
you that—as, to avoid accidents, I took the simple
precaution of filling all the dispensary-jars with
camphorated chalk—no serious results may be anti-

cipated from Dr. Herdal's rashness. [*Removes spec-tacles.*] Nora, don't you know me?

HILDA.

[*Reflects.*] I really don't remember having the pleasure——— And I'm *sure* I heard a harp in the air!

MRS. HERDAL.

I fancy, Miss Wangel, it must have been merely a bee in your bonnet

THE NEW ASSISTANT.

[*Tenderly.*] Still the same little singing-bird! Oh, Nora, my long-lost lark!

HILDA.

[*Sulkily.*] I'm *not* a lark—I'm a bird of prey—and when I get my claws into anything——— !

THE NEW ASSISTANT.

Macaroons, for instance? I remember your tastes of old. See, Nora! [*Produces a paper-bag from his coat-tail pocket.*] They were fresh this morning!

" My, my Pill-doctor ! "

HILDA.

[*Wavering.*] If you insist on·calling me Nora, I think you must be just a little mad yourself.

THE NEW ASSISTANT.

We are all a little mad—in Norway. But Torvald Helmer is sane enough still to recognise his own little squirrel again! Surely, Nora, your education is complete at last—you have gained the experience you needed ?

HILDA.

[*Nods slowly.*] Yes, Torvald, you're right enough *there.* I have thought things out for myself, and have got clear about them. And I have quite made up my mind that Society and the Law are all wrong, and that I am right.

HELMER.

[*Overjoyed.*] Then you *have* learnt the Great Lesson, and are fit to undertake the charge of your

children's education at last! You've no notion how
they've grown! Yes, Nora, our marriage will be a
true marriage now. You will come back to the
Dolls' House, won't you?

HILDA-NORA-HELMER-WANGEL.

[*Hesitates.*] Will you let me forge cheques if I do,
Torvald?

HELMER.

[*Ardently.*] All day. And at night, Nora, we will
falsify the accounts—together!

HILDA-NORA-HELMER-WANGEL.

[*Throws herself into his arms, and helps herself to
macaroons.*] That will be fearfully thrilling! My
—*my* Manager!

DR. HERDAL.

[*Comes out very pale, from dispensary.*] Hilda I
did take the—— I'm afraid I interrupt you?

HELMER.

Not in the least. But this lady is my little lark,

and she is going back to her cage by the next steamer.

Dr. Herdal.

[*Bitterly.*] Am I *never* to have a gleam of happiness? But stay—do I see my little Senna once more?

Rübub.

Pardon me—*my* little Senna. She always believed so firmly in my pill!

Dr. Herdal.

Well—well. If it must be. Rübub, I will take you into partnership, and we will take out a patent for that pill, jointly. Aline, my poor dear Aline, let us try once more if we cannot bring a ray of brightness into our cheerless home!

Mrs. Herdal.

Oh, Haustus, if only we *could*—but why do you propose that to me—*now?*

DR. HERDAL.

[*Softly—to himself.*] Because I have tried being a troll—and found that nothing came of it, and it wasn't worth sixpence!

> [HILDA-NORA *goes off to the right with* HELMER; SENNA *to the left with* RÜBUB; DR. HERDAL *and* MRS. HERDAL *sit on two of the galvanised-iron chairs, and shake their heads disconsolately as the* Curtain falls.

LITTLE MOPSËMAN

PERSONS

ALFRED FRÜYSECK (*Man of Letters*).

Mrs. SPRETA FRÜYSECK (*his wife*).

Little MOPSËMAN (*their Pudeldachs, six years
and nine months old*).

MOPSA BROVIK (*a little less than kin to* ALFRED).

Sanitary Engineer BLOCHDRÄHN.

The VARMINT-BLŌK.

LITTLE MOPSËMAN

THE FIRST ACT

A richly upholstered garden-room, full of art-pots and other furniture. MRS. SPRETA FRÖYSECK stands beside the table, unpacking the traditional bag. Shortly after, MISS MOPSA BROVIK enters by the door ; she carries a pink parasol and a rather portly portfolio with a patent lock.

MOPSA.

[*As she enters.*] Good morning, my dear Spreta! [*Sees the bag.*] Why, you are unpacking a travelling-bag on the drawing-room table! Then Alfred has actually come home?   [*Takes off her things.*

SPRETA.

[*Turns and nods with a teasing smile.*] As if you didn't *know!* When you have never been down in these parts all the time he has been away! [*Unpacking a flannel vest and a respirator.*] Yes, he turned up last night, quite unexpectedly.

MOPSA.

Then it was *that* that drew me out here! I felt I *must.* My poor dear mother, Kaia—she that was a Miss Fosli, you know—was like that. She always felt *she* must. It's heredity. Surely you can understand *that?*

SPRETA.

[*Takes out a bottle of cough mixture, and closes the bag with a snap.* I am not *quite* a fool, my dear.

But really, when you have such a firm admirer in
Mr. Blochdrähn——!

Mopsa.

He is such a mere bachelor. I never could feel
really attracted to any unmarried man. All that
seems to me so utterly unmaidenly. [*Changing the
subject.*] How *is* dear Alfred?

Spreta.

Dear Alfred is tired, but perfectly transfigured by
his trip. He has never once been away from me all
these years. Only think!

Mopsa.

That would account for it certainly. And I really
think he deserved some little outing. [*With an outburst of joy.*] Why, I shouldn't wonder if he has
positively finished his great big book while he has
been away!

Spreta.

[*With a half smile.*] Shouldn't you? *I* should.

But he has not mentioned it—perhaps he was too tired. And he has been trying to teach that miserable Little Mopsëman tricks ever since he came back. I never *did* care about dogs myself, and really Alfred is so perfectly absurd about him. Oh, here he is.

> [ALFRED FRÜYSECK *enters, followed by* LITTLE MOPSËMAN *on his hind legs.* ALFRED *is a weedy, thin-haired man of about thirty-five (or thirty-six) with tinted spectacles and limp side-whiskers.* MOPSËMAN *wears a military tunic and a shako very much over one eye, and is shouldering a small toy musket. He is bandy-legged, with a broad black snout and beautiful intelligent eyes. His tail is drooping and has lost all its hair.*

ALFRED.

[*Beaming.*] Just see what really wonderful progress Little Mopsëman has made already with his

drill. Why, my dearest Mopsa ! [*Goes up and kisses
her with marked pleasure.*] You have come here the
very morning after my return ? Fancy *that.*

Mopsa.

[*Gazes fixedly at him.*] I couldn't keep away.
You are looking quite splendid ! And how have you
got on with your wonderful large book, Alfred ? I
felt so sure it would go so easily when once you had
got away from dear Spreta.

Alfred.

[*Shrugging his shoulders.*] It *did*—wonderfully
easily. The truth is my thick fat book on *Canine
Idiosyncrasy*—h'm—has gone—entirely out of my
head. I have been trying thinking for a change.
It's easier than writing.

Spreta.

Yes, Alfred, I can understand that. And then,
when you had never really got farther than the
title——!

ALFRED.

[*Smiling at her.*] No farther than *that*. Somehow, none of the Früysecks ever *do*. My family is a thing apart. And now I have determined to devote my whole time to Little Mopsëman. I am going to foster all the noble germs in him, create a conscious happiness in his mind. [*With enthusiasm.*] That is my true vocation.

SPRETA.

You shouldn't have dressed the poor dog up like that. It does make him look so utterly ridiculous!

ALFRED.

[*Speaking lower and seriously.*] Only in the eyes of the Philistines who couldn't see any pathos in poor Mrs. Solness and her nine dolls. The truly reverent have no sense whatever of the ridiculous. Still, it would certainly be better in future to keep Little Mopsëman indoors, because if the dogs in the streets saw him in those clothes—[*clenching his hands*]—and after he has had that unfortunate accident to his tail, too!

Spreta.

Alfred, I won't *have* you bringing up that again! There's some one knocking. Come in.

The Varmint-Blōk.

[*Enters softly and noiselessly. He is a slouching, sinister figure, in a fur cap and a flowered comforter. He has a large green gingham in one hand, and in the other a bag which writhes unpleasantly.*] Humbly beg pardon, your worships, but you don't happen to feel in the humour to see how this little wounded warrior here—[*points to* Mopsëman]—would polish off the lovely little ratikins, do you?

Alfred.

[*With suppressed indignation.*] We most certainly do *not*. He is intended for higher things. Get out, you have frightened him under the sofa.

The Varmint-Blōk.

He'll come round right enough. . . . . There, didn't I *tell* you ! See how he sniffs at my legs. It's wonderful what a fancy dawgs *do* seem to take to me—follow me *anywhere*, they will. [*With a chuckling laugh.*] Seems as if they'd *got* to.

Spreta.

There is certainly no accounting—— And what becomes of them when they do?

The Varmint-Blōk.

[*With glittering eyes.*] Oh, *they're* safe enough, the sweet little creatures, lady. I'm very kind to 'em. And if I could only induce you to let your lovely poodlekin tackle a dozen rats, which 'ud be a holiday to a game little sportin' dawg like him—— *Not* this mornin'? then here's a loving good-day to you all, and thank ye kindly for nothing.

[*He backs out cringingly, as* Spreta *retires to the verandah, fanning herself elegantly*

" He backs out cringingly. . . . Mopseman slips out after him."

with her pocket-handkerchief; MOPSËMAN
slips out after him, unnoticed by all.
ALFRED *sees* MOPSA'S *portfolio.*

ALFRED.

[*To* MOPSA.] And have you positively lugged this
thing all the way out here. Wasn't it heavy?

MOPSA.

[*Nods.*] It *had* to be. It contains all the letters
written to my poor dear mother—by Master-builder
Solness, you know. My mother had such a rich,
beautiful past. I thought, Alfred, we might look
them through together quietly some evening, when
Spreta is out of the way.

[*Looks attentively at him.*

ALFRED.

[*Uneasily, to himself.*] Oh, my good gracious!
[*Aloud.*] It would certainly *have* to be some evening
when—— But on the whole, perhaps, I—I really

almost think we had better—— It isn't as if you
were *really* my second cousin !

Spreta.

[*Re-entering from verandah.*] Has that horrible
person with the rats gone ?   He has given me almost
a kind of turn.

Alfred.

He is a sort of itinerant Trope, I suppose.   Talking
of turns, did I tell you that I, too, have experienced
a kind of inward revolution away up there among the
peaks ? . . . I *have.*

Spreta.

Oh, heavens ! Alfred, was it the cookery at those
high mountain hotels ?

Alfred.

[*Soothingly, patting her head.*] Not altogether—be
very sure of *that.*   But it is rather a long story.   I
should recommend you to sit down.   [*They sit down*

expectantly.] I will try to tell you. [*Gazing straight before him.*] When I look back into the vague mists that enshroud my earliest infancy, I seem almost to——

SPRETA.

[*Slaps him.*] Oh, for goodness' sake, Alfred, do skip the introduction!

ALFRED.

[*Disappointed.*] It was the most interesting part! But the long and short of it is that I have resolved to renounce writing my wonderful work on *Canine Idiosyncrasy !* I am going to act it out instead—on Little Mopsëman. [*With shining eyes.*] I intend to perfect the rich possibilities that lie hidden in that rather unprepossessing poodle. *There !*

SPRETA.

[*Holding aloof from him.*] And is that *all !*

ALFRED.

H'm, yes, *that's* all. But you never *did* properly appreciate poor Little Mopsëman!

Mopsa.

[*Pressing his hand.*] She never did, Alfred. But *I*
do. And we will teach him the loveliest new tricks
together. • [*Fixes her eyes on him.*] Just you and I.

Spreta.

Alfred, I won't have the dog taught any tomfoolery.
You shall not divide yourself up like that. Do you
hear?

Sanitary Engineer Blochdrähn.

[*Enters by the door.*] Aha! so you've got your husband thoroughly in hand, as usual, eh, Mrs. Früyseck?
[*To the others.*] I bring glorious news. I have just
been called in to see to the Schoolhouse drains *again!*
I only laid them last Autumn; but there seems to
be a leakage somewhere. Quite a big piece of work,
really!

Mopsa.

And are you beaming with joy over *that?*

Sanitary Engineer Blochdrähn.

I am indeed. And afterwards I have several

important drains to disconnect at the great new hotel in Christiania, and the most tremendous scientific safeguards to grapple with and overthrow. What a glorious thing it is to be a plumber and make a little extra work for oneself in the world! Miss Mopsa, can I persuade you to to take a little turn in the garden? Do! *[Offers his arm.*

MOPSA.

[*Takes it.*] Oh, I don't mind—provided you don't talk shop or sentiment. *[They go out together.*

SPRETA.

[*Looks after them.*] What a pity it is that Mopsa can't take more to that Mr. Blochdrähn, *isn't* it, Alfred? *[Looks searchingly at him.*

ALFRED.

[*Wriggles.*] Oh—er—I don't know. For then we should see so much less of her.

SPRETA.

[*Vehemently.*] Oh, come! So much the better!

[*Clutching him round the neck.*] I want you all to myself, Alfred. I love you so much I could throttle you. I've a good mind to, as it is!

ALFRED.

[*Choking.*] You *are*. My loyal, proud, true-hearted Spreta, d-don't!   [*Gently releases himself.*

SPRETA.

You have ceased to care for me. Don't deny it, Alfred!   [*Bursts into convulsive weeping.*

ALFRED.

I will frankly admit that, like most married Norwegians, I am—h'm—subject to the Law of Change.

SPRETA.

[*With increasing excitement.*] I saw that so plainly last night. I sent out for some champagne, Alfred, expressly for *you*. And you didn't drink a drop of it!   [*Looks bitterly at him.*

ALFRED.

I knew the brand. [*With a gesture of repulsion.*] Gooseberry, my dear, gooseberry.

SPRETA.

You never even kissed me, either. But you can kiss *Mopsa !* Alfred, if you imagine *I* am the kind of person to play gooseberry——

ALFRED.

Need dramatic dialogue descend to these sordid details ? Really this is verging on mere vulgar logger-heads ! And when you know, too, how I have always regarded Mopsa almost as a sort of sister !

SPRETA.

I know that sort of sister, Alfred. She comes from Norway ! But I am none of your fish-blooded Mrs. Solnesses, or half-witted Beata Rosmers, and I'm not going to *stand* it ! I decline to share you with any-thing or anybody—whether it's a thick fat book that

never gets even begun, or a designing minx that helps
you in your precious " vocation," or a gorging little
mongrel, with his evil red and green eyes, that I'm
often tempted to wish at the bottom of the fiord !

[*Confused cries and barks are heard outside.*

ALFRED.

[*Shocked.*] Spreta ! When am I going to bring all
his desires into harmony with his digestion ! *How*
unkind of you ! [*Looks for a moment.*] What in the
world are all the dogs barking at down there ?

SANITARY ENGINEER BLOCHDRÄIIN.

[*Re-entering with* MOPSA, *by glass door.*] Only some
organ-grinder's monkey. They have just frightened it
into the fiord. *Such* fun !

ALFRED.

[*In an agony of dread.*] Can it be our Little——— ?
But he is burying bones in the back garden. And he
is not a *monkey*, either. And if he were, monkeys

can all swim. . . . What are they saying now ? . . .
Hush !

SANITARY ENGINEER BLOCHDRÄHN.

[*Leans over verandah railings.*] They say, " He is
still shouldering the little musket !"

ALFRED.

[*Almost paralysed.*] The little——it *is* Mopsëman !
I taught him to do it so thoroughly ! [*With out-
stretched arms.*] He cannot shoulder a musket and
swim too ! [*Glancing darkly at* SPRETA.] Woman,
you have your wish ! Henceforth my life will be one
long rankle of remorse ! [*Sinks down in the armchair.*

MOPSA.

[*With an affectionate expression in her eyes.*] Not
alone, Alfred ! We will rankle together—just you
and I.

ALFRED.

[*Rises half distracted.*] Oh my gracious goodness !
[*He rushes down into the garden.*

THE SECOND ACT

*A little narrow glen, with a slope in the background,
belonging to* ALFRED. *Under the dripping trees
a table and chairs, all made of thin birchstaves.
Everything is sodden with wet, and mist-wreaths
are driving about.* ALFRED FRÜYSECK, *dressed in
a black mackintosh, sits dejectedly on a chair.
Presently* MOPSA BROVIK *comes down the slope
cautiously behind, and touches his shoulder;*
ALFRED *jumps.*

MOPSA.

You shouldn't really sit about on damp seats in
such miserable weather, Alfred.   I have been hunting
for you everywhere.

[Closing her umbrella with quiet significance.

ALFRED.

[*To himself.*] Run to earth! Oh, Lor'! [*Aloud.*
If you would only be kind enough to search for
Mopsëman instead! I *cannot* unravel the mystery of
his disappearance. There he was, just entering upon
conscious intelligence—full of the infinite possibilities
of performing poodlehood. I had charged myself with
his education. After having been an usher at so
many boarding-schools, I felt peculiarly fitted for
such a task. And then a shady scoundrel has only
to come his way with rats in a bag——

MOPSA.

But we don't in the least know how it really all
came about.

ALFRED.

That infernal Varmint-Blōk is at the bottom of
it, you may depend upon that! Though what motive
in the world——[*Quivering.*] It's not as if Mopsëman
would ever have faced a rat. He used to bolt at the

mere sight of a blackbeetle even.   The whole thing is
so utterly meaningless, Mopsa.   And yet, I suppose
the order of the universe requires it.

MOPSA.

Have you indulged in these abstruse philosophical
speculations with Spreta?

ALFRED.

[*Shakes his head hopelessly.*] She is so utterly inca-
pable of——[MORSA *nods.*] I prefer discussing them
with *you.*   There is something unnatural in imparting
confidences to a mere wife.   What on earth have you
got there?

MOPSA.

[*Takes a little housewife from her pocket.*] Spreta
said you had lost the button off the back of your
collar.   I thought I would sew it on for you.   *May
I?* [*With quiet warmth.*] I'll *try* not to run the
needle into you.

ALFRED.

[*Absently.* Do; it may distract my thoughts a little. Where *is* Spreta, by the way?

MOPSA.

Only taking a little walk with Blochdrähn. [*Sewing.*] Perhaps it is *hardly* the weather for a stroll; but then he was always so perfectly devoted to—h'm—to Little Mopsëman, you know.

ALFRED.

[*Surprised.*] But Spreta wasn't. She never liked him—not even as a puppy. And now tell me—don't you think you could take a fancy to Blochdrähn—h'm?

MOPSA.

Oh, no! please! [*Covers her face with her hands.* You mustn't really ask me why. [*Looks at him through her fingers.*] Because I *know* I should tell you; you have such an irresistible influence over me! Oh dear! oh dear! what *will* you think of me? [*Moves

close up to him.]   There's a button off your *shirt-front*
now !

ALFRED.

[*Plaintively.*]   Am I to have *that* one sewn on too?

MORSA.

Yes, it's the right thing to do.   Though how Spreta
can *let* you go about like this, I *can't* think !

ALFRED.

[*With a half smile.*]   When I have *you* to look after
me.   This is quite like the dear old days !

MOPSA.

Yes.   [*Sewing.*]   I remembered I mended all your
things, like a sister.   Even then you never had *quite*
all your buttons, *had* you, dear ?

ALFRED.

[*Patting her head.*]   Not even then.   And do you
remember how you used to follow me about, just like
a little dog ?   And I used to call you " Little Mopsë-

man," because your name was Mopsa; and if I had had a dog I should have called *him* Little Mopsëman. And then how you used to sit up and hold a biscuit on your nose, my dear faithful Mopsa!

Mopsa.

I wonder how you can be so childish! [*Smiling involuntarily.*] It *was* a rich beautiful time; but it was all over when you married. I hope you have never mentioned all that nonsense to Spreta?

Alfred.

I *may* have. One *does* tell one's wife some things —unintentionally. [*Clutching his forehead.*] But oh, how *can* I sit here and forget Little Mopsëman so completely? Have I *no* heart?

Mopsa.

If you have lost it, I think I know where it is. And your must surely give you grief a rest occasionally, too.

ALFRED.

I mustn't. I won't. I *will* think of him. . . . . By
the way, are we to have dried fish for dinner *again ?*
. . . Oh, *there* I go once more—in the very middle
of my agony—just when I want to be torturing myself unspeakably with this gnawing crushing regret!
What a wonderfully realistic touch it is, though, eh ?
So dramatic ! But after all, I have *you*, Mopsa.   I'm
so glad of that !

MOPSA.

[*Looking earnestly at him.*] Surely you mean dear
Spreta—not *me*, Alfred ?

ALFRED.

What relation is a wife to her husband? None
whatever.   Now you, Mopsa, *you* are very nearly a
second cousin once removed, not quite—because our
family is a thing so entirely apart.   We have always
had vowels (the very *best* vowels) for our initials, and
the same coloured spectacles, and poor relations we

invariably cut and great thick works we never get
really on with. You take after your mother, Kaia.

Mopsa.

And my aunt—she that was a Miss Rebecca West.
I feel so irresistibly drawn to disturb other people's
domestic harmony. But you must really forget me,
and try to care for poor Spreta a little.

Alfred.

[*Vehemently.*] It's no use. I can't. You've en-
tranced me so thoroughly. [*Helplessly.*] I *know* you
would ! Do let me remain here with you !

[*Seizes her hand.*

Mopsa.

[*Looks warmly at him.*] Of course, if you really
mean *that*, I cannot pretend that such comradeship
is—— Hush ! let go my hand—there's somebody
coming !

SPRETA *and* BLOCHDRÄHN *enter in waterproofs,*
sharing the same umbrella.

ALFRED.

[*Annoyed.*] Why do you come bothering here?
Surely you must see that such an interruption is *most*
ill-timed.

SPRETA.

[*With a cutting laugh.*] We did gather *that*, Alfred.
I came to see what you were about.

ALFRED.

Mopsa was simply sympathising with me over Little
Mopsëman's disappearance—that was all.

SPRETA.

Sympathising and philandering, Alfred, are synony-
mous terms in the Norwegian Drama. And I may
be allowed to observe that *other* people can philander
if they're driven to it.   [*Glances at* BLOCHDRÄHN.

MOPSA.

[*Taking her umbrella quickly, to* BLOCHDRÄHN.] We
seem to be somewhat *de trop* here. Suppose we with-
draw?   [*They do.*

Spreta.

Doesn't it strike you, Alfred, that all this morbid harping on that missing mongrel may be just a little monotonous—for a popular audience, I mean?

Alfred.

[*Gloomily.*] They'll have to sit through another Act and a half of it—that's all. I shall harp if I choose. I *like* harping. And you always detested Mopsëman. You said he ate too much, and had evil eyes.

Spreta.

So he *did*—so he *had!* And *you* never really and truly loved him either, or you would never have made such a fool of the dog as you did!

Alfred.

I had renounced my wonderful thick book. I needed *something* to fill up my life.

Spreta.

You might have chosen something better than a miserable little poodle with no hair on his tail!

Q

ALFRED.

[*Turns pale.*] It is you—*you*, who were the guilty one in that. [*Harshly and coldly.*] It was *your* hand that spilt the hot water over him as he lay comfortably on the hearthrug. It *was!* And you *know* it!

SPRETA.

[*Terrified, yet defiant.*] Better own at once that you came behind me and jogged my arm!

ALFRED.

[*In suppressed desperation.*] Yes, that is true. You looked so entrancingly beautiful as you were putting the kettle on for tea, that I was irresistibly impelled to kiss you!

SPRETA.

[*Exasperated.*] Alfred! This is intolerable of you. *Do* I deserve to be reproached for looking entrancingly beautiful?

ALFRED.

[*With sarcasm.*] Not in the least—*now*. You are

subject to the Law of Change. But what does all that matter? We have *both* sinned, if you like. While we had him, we both shrank in secret from him—we could not bear to see the tail he dragged about after him !

SPRETA.

[*Whispers.*] You were so perpetually putting paraffin upon it, Alfred !

ALFRED.

[*Calmer.*] Yes, *that.* I tried to perfect its possibilities. But it was no use—I could never, never make it good again. And after that I dressed him up in military uniform, and then he had to remain too much indoors, so, of course, he followed the Varmint-Blök, and then the street curs chevied him over the pier. And after I had trained him so thoroughly to shoulder a musket, he was so totally unable to swim. Oh, it all works out into quite a logical Retribution. And I must go away into the solitudes and writhe with remorse—by myself.

SPRETA.

[*Bitingly.*] Unless, of course, you can induce Mopsa
to——I think you mentioned once that she used to
follow you about like a little dog?

ALFRED.

[*In a hollow voice.*] I did. I remember now. That
time when the tea-kettle—— Retribution!

> [*He staggers into the thinnest birchstave chair,
> which collapses under him.*

SPRETA.

[*Menacingly standing over him.*] Yes, Alfred, Retribution!   [MOPSA *and* BLOCHDRÄHN *return.*

MOPSA.

[*Pleasantly.*] Well, my dear Spreta, have you and
dear Alfred talked things thoroughly out?

SPRETA.

Oh, yes; quite thoroughly enough. I really will
not be left alone with Alfred any more; he is *too*
depressing!

" Yes, Alfred, Retribution ! "

ALFRED.

[*On the ground.*] One cannot be expected to rollick when one is being gnawed with remorse! But perhaps Blochdrähn *would* be a more cheerful companion for you; go on with him, while Mopsa helps me up again. We'll follow you—presently.

[SPRETA *and* BLOCHDRÄHN *go off together :*
    MOPSA *tenderly assists* ALFRED *to rise.*

MOPSA.

Oh, dear me! it does seem *such* a pity! But Spreta always *was* peculiar. It must be so trying for *you,* dear!

ALFRED.

So much so that I can't stand her any longer. I *must* get away, anywhere—quite alone. Mopsa, will you come *too?*

MOPSA.

[*Shocked.*] Alfred! How *can* you? What *have* I said or done to encourage such a proposal? So utterly unexpected!

ALFRED.

[*Feebly.*] I really couldn't help it. It's the troll inside me. What am I saying? That belongs to another Norwegian drama!

MOPSA.

All this part belongs to *several* other Norwegian dramas, dear. But we must see if we can't get out of the old groove *this* time!

ALFRED.

But why in the world——? When you showed such a wonderful preference for my society, too!

MOPSA.

[*Gently.*] I know, dear. But that was before—— Let me tell you something. [*Slow music;* ALFRED *sits down, cautiously.*] I've just been looking through my big portfolio, and I've discovered—what *do* you think? [ALFRED *shakes his head hopelessly.*] I'm not Kaia's daughter at all, really. I'm only adopted!

ALFRED.

But what difference does that make in *our* relations? Practically, none whatever !

MOPSA.

All the difference, Alfred. I always pursued you about with reluctance, and under protest. Being, as I supposed, descended from Kaia Fosli, and related to Rebecca West, it seemed so utterly the right thing to do. But I know *now* that I am nothing of the sort, and that if my real mother ever possessed such a thing as a Past at all, it was Plu-perfect. So heredity doesn't come in, and, rather than interfere between you and poor dear Sprota, I have decided to go right away and never see you again. I really *mean* it, *this* time !

[*She opens her umbrella and runs off up the slope.*

ALFRED.

[*Takes up his hat sadly.*] Isn't this play going to

end pessimistically after all, then ? [*Shudders.*] Are
we actually going to be—moral ? [*More hopefully.*]
After all, there's another Act left.   There's a chance
still !   [*He follows hastily after* MOPSA.

THE THIRD ACT

An elevation and rockery in FRÜYSECK'S *back-garden, from which—but for the houses in between—an extensive view over the steamer-pier and fiord could be obtained. In front, a summer-house, covered with creepers and wild earwigs. On a bench outside,* MOPSA *is sitting. She has the inevitable little travelling bag on a strap over her shoulder.* BLOCHDRÄHN *comes up in the dusk. He, too, has a travelling bag, made of straw, containing professional implements, over his shoulder. He is carrying a rolled up handbill and a small paste-pot.*

SANITARY ENGINEER BLOCHDRÄHN.

[*Catching sight of* MOPSA'S *hand-bag.*] So you really are off at last ? So am I. *I'm* going by train.

Mopsa.

[*With a faint smile.*] Are you? Then *I* take the steamer. Have you seen Alfred anywhere about—or Spreta?

Sanitary Engineer Blochdrähn.

I have been seeing a good deal of *Mrs.* Früyseck. She asked me to come up here and paste one of these handbills on the summer-house. To offer a reward for Little Mopsëman, you know. I've been sticking them up everywhere. [*Busied with the paste-pot.*] But you'll see—he'll never turn up.

Mopsa.

[*Sighing.*] Poor Spreta! and oh, poor *dear* Alfred! I really don't know if I *can* have the heart to leave him.

Sanitary Engineer Blochdrähn.

[*Pasting up the bill.*] I shall not believe it myself until I actually see you *do* it. But why shouldn't you come along with me, if you *are* going—h'm?

MOPSA.

If you were only a married man—but I have to be so careful *now*, you know !

SANITARY ENGINEER BLOCHDRÄHN.

It tortures me to think of our two handbags each taking its own way; it really does, Miss Mopsa. And then for me to have to plumb all by myself. Though, to be sure, one can always get round the district surveyor alone.

MOPSA.

Ah, yes, *that* you can surely manage alone.

SANITARY ENGINEER BLOCHDRÄHN.

But it takes two to connect the ventilating shaft with the main drainage.

MOPSA.

[*Looking up at him.*] Always two ? Never more ? Never many ?

SANITARY ENGINEER BLOCHDRÄHN.

Well, then, you see, it becomes quite a different

matter—it cuts down the profits.   But are you sure you can never make up your mind to share my great new job with me?

Mopsa.

I tried that once—with Alfred.   It didn't quite answer—though it was delightful, all the same.

Sanitary Engineer Blochdrähn.

Then there really *has* been a bright and happy time in your life?   I should never have suspected it !

Mopsa.

Oh, yes, you can't think how amusing Alfred was in those days.   When he distinguished himself by failing to pass his examinations, and then, from time to time, when he lost his post in some school or other; or when his big, bulky manuscripts were declined by some magazine—with thanks !

Sanitary Engineer Blochdrähn.

Yes, I can quite see that such an existence must

" It takes two to connect the ventilating shaft with the main drainage."

have had its moments of quiet merriment. [*Shaking his head.*] But I *don't* see what in the world possessed Alfred to go and marry as he did.

MOPSA.

[*With suppressed emotion.*] The Law of Change. Our latest catchphrase, you know. Alfred is so subject to it. So will *you* be, some day or other!

SANITARY ENGINEER BLOCHDRÄHN.

Never in all my life; whatever progress may be made in sanitation! [*Insistently.*] Can't you *really* care for me?

MOPSA.

I might—[*looking down*]—if you have no objection to go halves with Alfred.

SANITARY ENGINEER BLOCHDRÄHN.

I am behind the times, I daresay; but such an arrangement does *not* strike me as a firm basis for a really happy home. I should certainly object to it, most decidedly.

R

MOPSA.

[*Laughs bitterly.*] What creatures of convention you men are, after all! [*Recollecting herself.*] But I *quite* forgot. I am conventional *myself* now. You are perfectly right; it *would* be utterly irregular!

ALFRED.

[*Comes up the steps.*] Is it you, Blochdrähn, who posted up that bill? On the new summer-house!

SANITARY ENGINEER BLOCHDRÄHN.

Yes, Mrs. Früyseck asked me to.

ALFRED.

[*Touched.*] Then she *does* miss Little Mopsëman, after all! Are you going? Not without *Mopsa?*

SANITARY ENGINEER BLOCHDRÄHN.

[*Shaking his head.*] I did invite her to accompany me, but she won't. So I must do my jobs alone.

ALFRED.

It's so horrible to be alone; or *not* to be alone, if

it comes to that! [*Oppressed—to himself.*] My troll is
at it again! I shall press her to stay; I *know* I shall,
and it will end in the usual way!

SPRETA.

[*Comes up the steps, plaintirely.*] It *is* unkind of
you all to leave me alone like this. When I'm so
nervous in the dark, too!

MOPSA.

[*Tenderly.*] But I *must* leave you, Spreta, dear.
By the next steamer. That is—— Well, I really
ought to!

ALFRED.

[*Almost inaudibly, hitting himself on the chest.*]
Down, you little beggar, down! No, it's no use; the
troll *will* keep popping up! [*Aloud.*] Can't we persuade you, dear Mopsa? Do stay—just to keep
Spreta company, you know!

MOPSA.

[*As if struggling with herself.*] Oh, I want to so
much! I'd do *anything* to oblige dear Spreta

SANITARY ENGINEER BLOCHDRÄHN.

[*To himself, dejectedly.*] She is just like that Miss
Hilda Wangel for making herself so perfectly at
home!

SPRET A.

[*Resignedly.*] Oh, *I* don't mind. After all, I
would rather Alfred philandered than fretted and
fussed here alone with me. You had better stay,
and be our Little Mopsëman. It will keep Alfred
quiet—and that's *something!*

MOPSA.

No; it was only a temporary lapse. I keep on
forgetting that I am no longer an emotional Cuckoo
heroine. I am perfectly respectable; and I will
prove it by leaving with Mr. Blochdrähn at once—if
he will be so obliging as to escort me?

SANITARY ENGINEER BLOCHDRÄHN.

Delighted, my dear Miss Mopsa, at so unexpected
a bit of good luck. We've only just time to catch
the steamer.

Mopsa.

Then, thanks so much for a quite *too* delightful visit, Spreta. So *sorry* to have to run away like this ! [*To* Alfred, *with subdued anguish.*] I am running away—from *you!* I *entreat* you not to follow me — not *just* yet, at any rate !

Alfred.

[*Shrinking back.*] Ah ! [*To himself.*] If it depends upon our two trolls whether—— [Mopsa *goes off with* Sanitary Engineer Blochdräun.] There's the steamer, Spreta. . . . . By Jove, they'll have a run for it ! Look, she's putting in.

Spreta.

I daren't. The steamer has one red and one green eye—just like Mopsëman's at mealtimes !

Alfred.

[*Common-sensibly.*] Only her lights, you know. She doesn't mean anything *personal* by it.

SPRETA.

But they're actually mooring her by the very pier
that—— How can they have the *heart!*

ALFRED.

Steamboat companies have no feelings. Though
why *you* should feel it so, when you positively
loathed the dog.

SPRETA.

After all, you weren't so particularly fond of him
yourself; now *were* you, Alfred?

ALFRED.

H'm, he was a decent dog enough—for a mongrel.
I didn't *mind* him ; now you *did.*

SPRETA.

[*Nods slowly.*] There is a change in me now.   I
am easier to please.   I could share you with the
mangiest mongrel, if I were only quite sure you
would never again want to follow that minx Mopsa,
Alfred !

Alfred.

I never said I *did* want to ; though I can't answer
for the troll. But I must go away *somewhere* ; I'm
such a depressing companion for you. I shall go
away up into the solitudes—which reminds me of an
anecdote 1 never told either you or Mopsa before.
Sit down and I will tell it you.

Spreta.

[*Timidly.*] Not the one about the night of terror
you had on the mountains, Alfred, when you lost
your way and couldn't find a policeman anywhere
about the peaks ? Because I've heard *that*—and I
don't think I *can* stand it again.

Alfred.

[*Coldly and bitterly.*] You see that I have really
nothing to fill up my life with, when my own wife
refuses to listen to my anecdotes ! Now *Mopsa*
always—— What is all that barking down there in
the town ?

SPRETA.

[*With an outburst.*] Oh, you'll see, they've found
Little Mopsëman !

ALFRED.

Not they. He'll *never* be found. Those handbills
of yours were a mere waste of money. It is only the
curs fighting in the street—as usual.

SPRETA.

[*Slowly, and with resolution.*] Only that, Alfred.
And do you know what I mean to do, as soon as you
are away solitudinising up there in the mountain
hotels ? I will go down and bring all those poor
neglected dogs home with me.

ALFRED.

[*Uneasily.*] What—the whole *lot* of them, Spreta ?
[*Shocked.*] In our Little Mopsëman's place !

SPRETA.

[*Firmly and decidedly.*] Every one. To fill Little

Mopsëman's place. They shall dig up his bones, lie on his mat, take it in turns to sleep in his basket. I will try to—h'm—lighten and ennoble their lot in life.

ALFRED.

[*With growing uneasiness.*] When you simply detest all dogs! I don't know *any one* less fitted than you to manage a Dog's Home. I really don't!

SPRETA.

I must fill the void in my life *somehow*—if you go and leave me. And I must educate myself to *understand* dogs better, that's all.

ALFRED.

Yes, that you would *have* to do. [*As if struck with an idea.*] Before you *begin*. Suppose I take up my big fat book on *Canine Idiosyncrasy* once more, eh? That would teach you how to purify and ennoble every poodle really scientifically, you know. Only you must promise to wait till I've got it *done*.

SPRETA.

[*With a melancholy smile.*] I am in no hurry, Alfred. Only to write that you would have to remain at home.

ALFRED.

[*Half evasively.*] Not necessarily. I *might*, of course—for a while, that is. But I shall have many a heavy day of work before me, Spreta, and you will see, now and then perhaps, a great slumberous peace descend on me as I toil away in my brown study— but I shall be making wonderful progress all the same.

SPRETA.

I shall quite understand *that*, Alfred. Oh, dear, who in the world's this?

The VARMINT-BLÖK *appears mysteriously
in the gloom.*

THE VARMINT-BLÖK.

Excuse me, Captin, and your sweet ladyship, but I just happened to drop my eye on one of those lovely little hand-billikins here, and took the liberty to step up, thinking it might so happen that you'd been advertising the very identical dawg what followed me home the other day. You may remember me passing the remark how wonderful partial dawgs was to me. So I brought him up on the chance like.

[*He produces* LITTLE MOPSËMAN—*in mufti— from a side-pocket.*

SPRETA.

It *is* our Little Mopseman! So you are *not* some supernatural sort of shadowy symbol after all, then?

THE VARMENT-BLOK.

[*Hurt.*] Now I ask you, lady—do I look it? Here's my professional card. And if you *should* have the reward handy——[*As* ALFRED *pays him.*] Five Rix dollarkins—correct, my lord, and thankee kindly. [*As he departs.*] You'll find I've learned that sweet little mongrel a thing or two; take the nonsense out of any rat in Norway *now*, he will.

And just you ask him to set up and give three cheers for Dr. Ibsen—that's all !

> [*He goes out, chuckling softly.*

ALFRED.

[*Holding out* LITTLE MOPSĒMAN *at arms' length.*] H'm ; it will be a heavy day's work to purify and ennoble this poodle after all he has been through, eh, Spreta ? I think, as you seem to have developed quite a taste for such tasks, I shall allow *you* to undertake it—all by yourself.

SPRETA.

[*Turns away with her half-teasing smile.*] Thanks !

THE END.

Printed by BALLANTYNE, HANSON & CO.
London and Edinburgh.

𝕿𝖊𝖑𝖊𝖌𝖗𝖆𝖕𝖍𝖎𝖈 𝕬𝖉𝖉𝖗𝖊𝖘𝖘,
𝕾𝖚𝖓𝖑𝖔𝖈𝖐𝖘, 𝕷𝖔𝖓𝖉𝖔𝖓.

21 BEDFORD STREET, W.C.

March 1895.

A LIST OF

Mr WILLIAM HEINEMANN'S

PUBLICATIONS

.

MASTERPIECES OF GREEK SCULPTURE.

A SERIES OF ESSAYS ON THE HISTORY OF ART.

BY ADOLF FURTWÄNGLER.

Authorised Translation.   Edited by EUGÉNIE SELLERS.

With 19 full-page and 200 text Illustrations..   In One Volume.

4to, cloth, £3 3s. net.

*** Also an *édition de luxe* on Japanese vellum, limited to 50 numbered copies. In Two Volumes, price £10 10s. net.

The TIMES.—"In very many ways the translation is an improvement on the original. We sincerely hope it will be read by English students in the Universities and elsewhere."

The ST. JAMES'S GAZETTE.—"Not alone students of archæology, but artists, and collectors of choice books will revel in this sumptuous volume. The fine series of masterpieces of Greek sculpture here faultlessly reproduced is unequalled, whether in instructive arrangement or in perfection of the mechanical process. The illustrations are, almost without exception, photographically reproduced from the statues themselves (either the originals or casts), and we thus obtain the maximum of exact fidelity.

" But this is much more than a book of beautiful pictures : it is a critical study of the chief schools of Greek sculpture in its highest development by a scholar of acknowledged authority. No more suggestive or, to students, fascinating essays on Greek art have appeared for many years ; nothing so comprehensive and at the same time so strictly *first-hand* has been achieved since the days of Winckleman, or at least K. O. Müller ; though it is obvious that without the guiding influence of the late but ever-to-be lamented Brunn no such minute critical study would have been possible.

" Miss Sellers' edition is in every way a real improvement upon the original German edition of a year or two ago. She has rearranged the materials, and thus achieved a lucidity and continuity of argument which were much less conspicuous in the German."

The DAILY CHRONICLE.—"The fame of these masterly essays has grown in Germany since their first appearance to such a point that even in that country of learned rivalries they are admitted to be a paramount authority in their own sphere."

REMBRANDT:
SEVENTEEN OF HIS MASTERPIECES
FROM THE COLLECTION OF HIS PICTURES IN THE CASSEL GALLERY.

Reproduced in Photogravure by the Berlin Photographic Company.

WITH AN ESSAY

By FREDERICK WEDMORE.

In large portfolio 27½ inches × 20 inches.

The first twenty-five impressions of each plate are numbered and signed, and of these only fourteen are for sale in England at the net price of Twenty Guineas the set. The price of the impressions after the first twenty-five is Twelve Guineas net, per set.

The TIMES.—"The renderings have been made with extreme care, and, printed as they are upon peculiarly soft Japanese paper, they recall in a remarkable way the richness and beauty of the originals."

REMBRANDT:
HIS LIFE, HIS WORK, AND HIS TIME.

BY

ÉMILE MICHEL,
MEMBER OF THE INSTITUTE OF FRANCE.

TRANSLATED BY

FLORENCE SIMMONDS.

EDITED AND PREFACED BY

FREDERICK WEDMORE.

A re-issue in 16 Monthly Parts, price 2s. 6d. net, per Part.

⁎ A few copies of the FIRST EDITION are still on sale, price £2 2s. net; also of the EDITION DE LUXE (printed on Japanese vellum with India proof duplicates of the photogravures), price £12 12s. net.

The TIMES.—"This very sumptuous and beautiful book has long been expected by all students of Rembrandt, for M. Émile Michel, the chief French authority on the Dutch School of Painting, has been known to be engaged upon it for many years. . . . . Merely to look through the reproductions in M. Michel's book is enough to explain the passionate eagerness with which modern collectors carry on their search after Rembrandt's drawings, and the great prices which are paid for them."

COREA, or CHO-SEN,
THE LAND OF THE MORNING CALM.
By A. HENRY SAVAGE-LANDOR.

With 38 Illustrations from Drawings by the Author, and a Portrait.
Demy 8vo, 18s.

The Realm.—"Mr. Landor's book . . . . is of extreme value, for he has used his eyes, his pen, and his brush to picture scenes and natural characteristics, which in all probability will be vastly modified by the events of the immediate years."

The Morning Post.—"The book contains a great deal of matter which is entirely new, and cannot fail to attract considerable attention at the present time, when so little is known about Corea and the Coreans."

CORRECTED IMPRESSIONS.
ESSAYS ON VICTORIAN WRITERS.
By GEORGE SAINTSBURY.

Crown 8vo, gilt top, 7s. 6d.

The Times.—"He knows that in thirty years the general opinion has had time to clarify itself and to assimilate itself more or less to the more instructed opinion of the wise and the select. . . . . From this point of view there is not a little to be said for Mr. Saintsbury's method ; his application of it is . . . . instructive."

DEGENERATION.
By MAX NORDAU.

Translated from the Second Edition of the German work.
In One Volume, demy 8vo, 17s. net.

The Standard.—"A most suggestive, a most learned, and (may we add ?) a most entertaining volume."

The Daily Chronicle.—"A powerful, trenchant, savage attack on all the leading literary and artistic idols of the time by a man of great intellectual power, immense range of knowledge, and the possessor of a lucid style. . . . . This remarkable and stirring book, which is sure to be vehemently attacked, but which cannot be ignored."

A 2

Recent Publications.

MY PARIS NOTE-BOOK. By the Author of "An Englishman in Paris." In One Volume, demy 8vo. Price 14s.

The Daily Telegraph.—"One of those exceptionally delightful books the
manifold fascinations of which it is difficult to exemplify by quotation."

Galignani's Messenger.—"Want of space forbids us to make further
quotations from the good things in which the book abounds."

EDMUND AND JULES DE GONCOURT. Letters and
Leaves from their Journals. Selected. In Two Volumes, 8vo. With
Eight Portraits, 32s.

The Realm.—"It is impossible to indicate the immense variety of entertaining and often profoundly interesting matter which these volumes contain."

MEMOIRS (VIEUX SOUVENIRS) OF THE PRINCE
DE JOINVILLE. Translated from the French by Lady MARY LOYD.
With 78 Illustrations from drawings by the Author. In One Volume,
demy 8vo, 15s. net.

The Times.—"They are written in the breezy style of a sailor."

The St. James's Gazette.—"This is one of the most entertaining volumes of
memoirs that have appeared within recent years."

The Glasgow Herald.—"A very storehouse of anecdotes and incidents that
carry the reader along, and have all the charm of a bright and sparkling conversation."

NAPOLEON AND THE FAIR SEX. (Napoleon et les
Femmes). From the French of FRÉDÉRIC MASSON. In One Volume,
demy 8vo. With Ten Portraits, 15s. net.

The Daily Chronicle.—"The author shows that this side of Napoleon's
life must be understood by those who would realize the manner of man he was."

THE STORY OF A THRONE. Catherine II. of Russia.
From the French of K. WALISZEWSKI, Author of "The Romance of an
Empress." With a Portrait. In Two Volumes, demy 8vo, 28s.

The World.—"No novel that ever was written could compete with this
historical monograph in absorbing interest."

THE ROMANCE OF AN EMPRESS. Catherine II. of
Russia. By K. WALISZEWSKI. Translated from the French. Second
Edition. In One Volume, 8vo. With Portrait. Price 7s. 6d.

The Times.—"This book is based on the confessions of the Empress herself; it gives striking pictures of the condition of the contemporary Russia
which she did so much to mould as well as to expand. . . . Few stories in
history are more romantic than that of Catherine II. of Russia, with its
mysterious incidents and thrilling episodes ; few characters present more curious
problems."

A FRIEND OF THE QUEEN. Marie Antoinette and
Count Fersen. By PAUL GAULOT. Translated from the French by
Mrs. CASHEL HOEY. In Two Volumes, 8vo. With Two Portraits.
Price 24s.

The Times.—" M. Gaulot's work tells, with new and authentic details, the
romantic story of Count Fersen's devotion to Marie Antoinette, of his share in
the celebrated Flight to Varennes and in many other well-known episodes of
the unhappy Queen's life."

ALEXANDER III. OF RUSSIA. By CHARLES LOWE,
M.A., Author of "Prince Bismarck : an Historical Biography." Crown
8vo, with Portrait in Photogravure, 6s.

The Athenæum.—" A most interesting and valuable volume."
The Academy.—" Written with great care and strict impartiality."

PRINCE BISMARCK. An Historical Biography. By
CHARLES LOWE, M.A. With Portraits. Crown 8vo, 6s.

VILLIERS DE L'ISLE ADAM : His Life and Works.
From the French of VICOMTE ROBERT DU PONTAVICE DE HEUSSEY.
By Lady MARY LOYD. With Portrait and Facsimile. Crown 8vo, cloth,
10s. 6d.

THE LIFE OF HENRIK IBSEN. By HENRIK JÆGER.
Translated by CLARA BELL. With the Verse done into English from the
Norwegian Original by EDMUND GOSSE. Crown 8vo, cloth, 6s.

RECOLLECTIONS OF MIDDLE LIFE. By FRANCISQUE
SARCEY. Translated by E. L. CAREY. In One Volume, 8vo. With
Portrait. 10s. 6d.

TWENTY-FIVE YEARS IN THE SECRET SERVICE.
The Recollections of a Spy. By Major HENRI LE CARON. With New
Preface. 8vo, boards, price 2s. 6d., or cloth, 3s. 6d.

*** *The Library Edition, with Portraits and Facsimiles, 8vo. 14s., is still
on sale.*

THE FAMILY LIFE OF HEINRICH HEINE. Illus-
trated by one hundred and twenty-two hitherto unpublished letters ad-
dressed by him to different members of his family. Edited by his nephew,
Baron LUDWIG VON EMBDEN, and translated by CHARLES GODFREY
LELAND. In One Volume, 8vo, with 4 Portraits. 12s. 6d.

RECOLLECTIONS OF COUNT LEO TOLSTOY.
Together with a Letter to the Women of France on the "Kreutzer
Sonata." By C. A. BEHRS. Translated from the Russian by C. E.
TURNER, English Lecturer in the University of St. Petersburg. In One
Volume, 8vo. With Portrait. 10s. 6d.

QUEEN JOANNA I. OF NAPLES, SICILY, AND
JERUSALEM ; Countess of Provence, Forcalquier, and Piedmont. An
Essay on her Times. By ST. CLAIR BADDELEY. Imperial 8vo. With
Numerous Illustrations. 16s.

CHARLES III. OF NAPLES AND URBAN VI.; also
CECCO D'ASCOLI, Poet, Astrologer, Physican. Two Historical Essays.
By St. Clair Baddeley. With Illustrations, 8vo, cloth, 10s. 6d.

DE QUINCEY MEMORIALS. Being Letters and other
Records here first Published, with Communications from Coleridge, The
Wordsworths, Hannah More, Professor Wilson, and others. Edited
with Introduction, Notes, and Narrative, by Alexander H. Japp, LL.D.,
F.R.S.E. In two volumes, demy 8vo, cloth, with Portraits, 30s. net.

MEMOIRS. By Charles Godfrey Leland (Hans Breitmann). Second Edition. In One Volume, 8vo. With Portrait. Price
7s. 6d.

ALFRED, LORD TENNYSON. A Study of His Life and
Work. By Arthur Waugh, B.A. Oxon. With Twenty Illustrations
from Photographs specially taken for this Work. Five Portraits, and
Facsimile of Tennyson's MS. Crown 8vo, cloth, gilt edges, or uncut, 6s.

THE PROSE WORKS OF HEINRICH HEINE.
Translated by Charles Godfrey Leland, M.A., F.R.L.S. (Hans
Breitmann). In Eight Volumes.

The Library Edition, in crown 8vo, cloth, at 5s. per volume. Each volume of
this edition is sold separately. The Cabinet Edition, in special binding,
boxed, price £2 10s. the set. The Large Paper Edition, limited to 100
Numbered Copies, price 15s. per volume net, will only be supplied to
subscribers for the Complete Work.

I. FLORENTINE NIGHTS, SCHNABELEWOPSKI,
THE RABBI OF BACHARACH, and SHAKE-
SPEARE'S MAIDENS AND WOMEN.

II., III. PICTURES OF TRAVEL. 1823-1828.

IV. THE SALON. Letters on Art, Music, Popular Life,
and Politics.

V., VI. GERMANY.

VII., VIII. FRENCH AFFAIRS. Letters from Paris 1832,
and Lutetia.

THE POSTHUMOUS WORKS OF THOMAS DE
QUINCEY. Edited with Introduction and Notes from the Author's
Original MSS., by Alexander H. Japp, LL.D, F.R.S.E., &c. Crown
8vo, cloth, 6s. each.

I. SUSPIRIA DE PROFUNDIS. With other Essays.

II. CONVERSATION AND COLERIDGE. With other
Essays.

A COMMENTARY ON THE WORKS OF HENRIK

IBSEN. By HJALMAR HJORTH BOYESEN, Author of "Goethe and Schiller," "Essays on German Literature," &c. Crown 8vo, cloth, 7s. 6d. net.

THE JEW AT HOME. Impressions of a Summer and

Autumn Spent with Him in Austria and Russia. By JOSEPH PENNELL. With Illustrations by the Author. 4to, cloth, 5s.

THE NEW EXODUS. A Study of Israel in Russia. By

HAROLD FREDERIC. Demy 8vo, Illustrated, 16s.

THE GREAT WAR OF 189—. A Forecast. By Rear-

Admiral COLOMB, Col. MAURICE, R.A., Captain MAUDE, ARCHIBALD FORBES, CHARLES LOWE, D. CHRISTIE MURRAY, and F. SCUDAMORE. In One Volume, large 8vo. With numerous Illustrations, 12s. 6d.

THE COMING TERROR. And other Essays and Letters.

By ROBERT BUCHANAN. Second Edition. Demy 8vo, cloth, 12s. 6d.

STUDIES OF RELIGIOUS HISTORY. By ERNEST

RENAN, late of the French Academy. In One Volume, 8vo, 7s. 6d.

THE ARBITRATOR'S MANUAL. Under the London

Chamber of Arbitration. Being a Practical Treatise on the Power and Duties of an Arbitrator, with the Rules and Procedure of the Court of Arbitration, and the Forms. By JOSEPH SEYMOUR SALAMAN, Author of "Trade Marks," &c. Fcap. 8vo, 3s. 6d.

MANNERS, CUSTOMS, AND OBSERVANCES: Their

Origin and Signification. By LEOPOLD WAGNER. Crown 8vo, 6s.

ARABIC AUTHORS: A Manual of Arabian History and

Literature. By F. F. ARBUTHNOT, M.R.A.S., Author of "Early Ideas," "Persian Portraits," &c. 8vo, cloth, 5s.

THE LABOUR MOVEMENT IN AMERICA. By

RICHARD T. ELY, Ph.D., Associate in Political Economy, Johns Hopkins University. Crown 8vo, cloth, 5s.

THE SPEECH OF MONKEYS. By Professor R. L.

GARNER. Crown 8vo, 7s. 6d.

THE PASSION PLAY AT OBERAMMERGAU, 1890.

By F. W. FARRAR, D.D., F.R.S., Archdeacon and Canon of Westminster, &c. &c. 4to, cloth, 2s. 6d.

THE WORD OF THE LORD UPON THE WATERS

Sermons read by His Imperial Majesty the Emperor of Germany, while at Sea on his Voyages to the Land of the Midnight Sun. Composed by Dr. RICHTER, Army Chaplain, and Translated from the German by JOHN R. McILRAITH. 4to, cloth, 2s. 6d.

THE KINGDOM OF GOD IS WITHIN YOU.

Christianity not as a Mystic Religion but as a New Theory of Life. By COUNT LEO TOLSTOY. Translated from the Russian by CONSTANCE GARNETT. Library Edition, in two volumes, crown 8vo, 10s. Also a Popular Edition in One Volume, cloth, 2s. 6d.

MR. PUNCH'S POCKET IBSEN.

A Collection of some of the Master's best known Dramas, condensed, revised, and slightly re-arranged for the benefit of the Earnest Student. By F. ANSTEY, Author of "Vice Versa," "Voces Populi," &c. With Illustrations, reproduced by permission, from *Punch*, and a new Frontispiece, by Bernard Partridge. 16mo, cloth, 3s. 6d.

FROM WISDOM COURT.

By HENRY SETON MERRIMAN and STEPHEN GRAHAM TALLENTYRE. With 30 Illustrations by E. COURBOIN. Crown 8vo, cloth, 3s. 6d.

THE OLD MAIDS' CLUB.

By I. ZANGWILL, Author of "Children of the Ghetto," &c. Illustrated by F. H. TOWNSEND. Crown 8vo, cloth, 3s. 6d.

WOMAN—THROUGH A MAN'S EYEGLASS.

By MALCOLM C. SALAMAN. With Illustrations by DUDLEY HARDY. Crown 8vo, cloth, 3s. 6d.

STORIES OF GOLF.

Collected by WILLIAM KNIGHT and T. T. OLIPHANT. With Rhymes on Golf by various hands; also Shakespeare on Golf, &c. *Enlarged Edition.* Fcap. 8vo, cloth, 2s. 6d.

GIRLS AND WOMEN.

By E. CHESTER. Pott 8vo, cloth, 2s. 6d., or gilt extra, 3s. 6d.

QUESTIONS AT ISSUE.

Essays. By EDMUND GOSSE. Crown 8vo, buckram, gilt top, 7s. 6d.

*** *A Limited Edition on Large Paper*, 25s. *net.*

GOSSIP IN A LIBRARY.

By EDMUND GOSSE, Author of "Northern Studies," &c. Third Edition. Crown 8vo, buckram, gilt top, 7s. 6d.

*** *A Limited Edition on Large Paper*, 25s. *net.*

THE ROSE : A Treatise on the Cultivation, History, Family Characteristics, &c., of the Various Groups of Roses. With Accurate Description of the Varieties now Generally Grown. By H. B. ELL-WANGER. With an Introduction by GEORGE H. ELLWANGER. 12mo, cloth, 5*s.*

THE GARDEN'S STORY; or, Pleasures and Trials of an Amateur Gardener. By G. H. ELLWANGER. With an Introduction by the Rev. C. WOLLEY DOD. 12mo, cloth, with Illustrations, 5*s.*

THE GENTLE ART OF MAKING ENEMIES. As pleasingly exemplified in many instances, wherein the serious ones of this earth, carefully exasperated, have been prettily spurred on to indiscretions and unseemliness, while overcome by an undue sense of right. By J. M'NEILL WHISTLER. *A New Edition.* Pott 4to, half-cloth, 10*s.* 6*d.*

A CATALOGUE OF THE ACCADEMIA DELLE BELLE ARTI AT VENICE. With Biographical Notices of the Painters and Reproductions of some of their Works. Edited by E. M. KEARY. Crown 8vo, cloth, 2s. 6d. net ; paper, 2s. net.

THE HOURS OF RAPHAEL, IN OUTLINE. Together with the Ceiling of the Hall where they were originally painted. By MARY E. WILLIAMS. Folio, cloth, £2 2*s.* net,

---

Books for Presentation.

A BATTLE AND A BOY. By BLANCHE WILLIS HOWARD. With Thirty-nine Illustrations by A. MAC-NIELL-BARBOUR. Crown 8vo, cloth gilt, 6s.

THE ATTACK ON THE MILL. By EMILE ZOLA. With Twenty-one Illustrations, and Five exquisitely printed Coloured Plates, from original drawings by E. COURBOIN. In One Volume. 4to, 5s.

LITTLE JOHANNES. By F. VAN EEDEN. Translated from the Dutch by CLARA BELL. With an Introduction by ANDREW LANG. In One Volume. 16mo. Cloth, silver top, 3s. net.

THE LITTLE MANX NATION. (Lectures delivered at the Royal Institution, 1891.) By HALL CAINE, Author of "The Bondman," "The Scapegoat," &c. Crown 8vo, cloth, 3s. 6d.; paper, 2s. 6d.

NOTES FOR THE NILE. Together with a Metrical Rendering of the Hymns of Ancient Egypt and of the Precepts of Ptahhotep (the oldest book in the world). By HARDWICKE D. RAWNSLEY, M.A. Imperial 16mo, cloth, 5s.

DENMARK: its History, Topography, Language, Literature, Fine Arts, Social Life, and Finance. Edited by H. WEITEMEYER. Demy 8vo, cloth, with Map, 12s. 6d.
. *Dedicated, by permission, to H.R.H. the Princess of Wales.*

THE REALM OF THE HABSBURGS. By SIDNEY WHITMAN, Author of "Imperial Germany." In One Volume. Crown 8vo, 7s. 6d.

IMPERIAL GERMANY. A Critical Study of Fact and Character. By SIDNEY WHITMAN. New Edition, Revised and Enlarged. Crown 8vo, cloth, 2s. 6d.; paper, 2s.

THE CANADIAN GUIDE-BOOK. Part I. The Tourist's and Sportsman's Guide to Eastern Canada and Newfoundland, including full descriptions of Routes, Cities, Points of Interest, Summer Resorts, Fishing Places, &c., in Eastern Ontario, The Muskoka District, The St. Lawrence Region, The Lake St. John Country, The Maritime Provinces, Prince Edward Island, and Newfoundland. With an Appendix giving Fish and Game Laws, and Official Lists of Trout and Salmon Rivers and their Lessees. By CHARLES G. D. ROBERTS, Professor of English Literature in King's College, Windsor, N.S. With Maps and many Illustrations. Crown 8vo, limp cloth, 6s.

Part II. **WESTERN CANADA.** Including the Peninsula and Northern Regions of Ontario, the Canadian Shores of the Great Lakes, the Lake of the Woods Region, Manitoba and "The Great North-West," The Canadian Rocky Mountains and National Park, British Columbia, and Vancouver Island. By ERNEST INGERSOLL. With Maps and many Illustrations. Crown 8vo, limp cloth, 6s.

THE GUIDE-BOOK TO ALASKA AND THE NORTH-WEST COAST, including the Shores of Washington, British Columbia, South-Eastern Alaska, the Aleutian and the Seal Islands, the Behring and the Arctic Coasts. By E. R. SCIDMORE. With Maps and many Illustrations. Crown 8vo, limp cloth, 6s.

THE GENESIS OF THE UNITED STATES. A Narrative of the Movement in England, 1605-1616, which resulted in the Plantation of North America by Englishmen, disclosing the Contest between England and Spain for the Possession of the Soil now occupied by the United States of America; set forth through a series of Historical Manuscripts now first printed, together with a Re-issue of Rare Contemporaneous Tracts, accompanied by Bibliographical Memoranda, Notes, and Brief Biographies. Collected, Arranged, and Edited by ALEXANDER BROWN, F.R.H.S. With 100 Portraits, Maps, and Plans. In two volumes. Royal 8vo, buckram, £3 13s. 6d.

IN THE TRACK OF THE SUN. Readings from the Diary of a Globe-Trotter. By FREDERICK DIODATI THOMPSON. With many Illustrations by Mr HARRY FENN and from Photographs. In one volume 4to, 25s.

Dramatic Literature.

THE SECOND MRS. TANQUERAY. A Play in Four Acts. By ARTHUR W. PINERO. Small 4to, cloth, with a new Portrait of the Author, 5*s.*

LITTLE EYOLF. A Play in Three Acts. By HENRIK IBSEN. Translated from the Norwegian by WILLIAM ARCHER. Small 4to, cloth, with Portrait, 5*s.*

THE MASTER BUILDER. A Play in Three Acts. By HENRIK IBSEN. Translated from the Norwegian by EDMUND GOSSE and WILLIAM ARCHER. Small 4to, with Portrait, 5*s.* Popular Edition, paper, 1*s.* Also a Limited Large Paper Edition, 21*s.* net.

HEDDA GABLER : A Drama in Four Acts. By HENRIK IBSEN. Translated from the Norwegian by EDMUND GOSSE. Small 4to, cloth, with Portrait, 5*s.* Vaudeville Edition, paper, 1*s.* Also a Limited Large Paper Edition, 21*s.* net.

BRAND : A Dramatic Poem in Five Acts. By HENRIK IBSEN. Translated in the original metres, with an Introduction and Notes, by C. H. HERFORD. Small 4to, cloth, 7*s.* 6*d.*

HANNELE : A DREAM-POEM. By GERHART HAUPT-MANN. Translated by WILLIAM ARCHER. Small 4to, with Portrait, 5*s.* To be followed by

LONELY FOLK and **THE WEAVERS.**

THE PRINCESSE MALEINE : A Drama In Five Acts (Translated by Gerard Harry), and THE INTRUDER : A Drama in One Act. By MAURICE MAETERLINCK. With an Introduction by HALL CAINE, and a Portrait of the Author. Small 4to, cloth, 5*s.*

THE FRUITS OF ENLIGHTENMENT : A Comedy in Four Acts. By Count LYOF TOLSTOY. Translated from the Russian by E. J. DILLON. With Introduction by A. W. PINERO. Small 4to, with Portrait, 5*s.*

KING ERIK. A Tragedy. By EDMUND GOSSE. A Re-issue, with a Critical Introduction by Mr. THEODORE WATTS. Fcap. 8vo, boards, 5*s.* net.

THE PIPER OF HAMELIN. A Fantastic Opera in Two Acts. By ROBERT BUCHANAN. With Illustrations by HUGH THOMSON. 4to, cloth, 2*s.* 6*d.* net.

HYPATIA. A Play in Four Acts. Founded on CHARLES KINGSLEY's Novel. By G. STUART OGILVIE. With Frontispiece by J. D. BATTEN. Crown 8vo, cloth, printed in Red and Black, 2*s.* 6*d.* net.

THE DRAMA : ADDRESSES. By HENRY IRVING. With Portrait by J. McN. Whistler. Second Edition. Fcap. 8vo, 3*s.* 6*d.*

SOME INTERESTING FALLACIES OF THE Modern Stage. An Address delivered to the Playgoers' Club at St. James's Hall, on Sunday, 6th December 1891. By HERBERT BEERBOHM TREE. Crown 8vo, sewed, 6*d.* net.

THE PLAYS OF ARTHUR W. PINERO. With Introductory Notes by MALCOLM C. SALAMAN. 16mo, paper covers, 1*s.* 6*d.*; or cloth, 2*s.* 6*d.*

I. THE TIMES.
II. THE PROFLIGATE.
III. THE CABINET MINISTER.
IV. THE HOBBY HORSE.
V. LADY BOUNTIFUL.
VI. THE MAGISTRATE.
VII. DANDY DICK.

VIII. SWEET LAVENDER.
IX. THE SCHOOL-MISTRESS.
X. THE WEAKER SEX.
XI. LORDS AND COMMONS.
XII. THE SQUIRE.

Poetry.

IN RUSSET AND SILVER. POEMS. By EDMUND
GOSSE. Author of "Gossip in a Library," &c. In One Volume.
Crown 8vo, buckram, gilt top, 6s.

A CENTURY OF GERMAN LYRICS. Translated from
the German by KATE FREILIGRATH KROEKER. Fcap. 8vo, rough
edges, 3s. 6d.

LOVE SONGS OF ENGLISH POETS, 1500–1800.
With Notes by RALPH H. CAINE. Fcap. 8vo, rough edges, 3s. 6d.
** *Large Paper Edition, limited to 100 Copies,* 10s. 6d. net.

IVY AND PASSION FLOWER: Poems. By GERARD
BENDALL, Author of "Estelle," &c. &c.   12mo, cloth, 3s. 6d.
Scotsman.—"Will be read with pleasure."
Musical World.—"The poems are delicate specimens of art, graceful and
polished."

VERSES. By GERTRUDE HALL. 12mo, cloth, 3s. 6d.
Manchester Guardian.—"Will be welcome to every lover of poetry who
takes it up."

IDYLLS OF WOMANHOOD. By C. AMY DAWSON.
Fcap. 8vo, gilt top, 5s.

TENNYSON'S GRAVE. By ST. CLAIR BADDELEY. 8vo,
paper, 1s.

Heinemann's Scientific Handbooks.

MANUAL OF BACTERIOLOGY. By A. B. GRIFFITHS,
Ph.D., F.R.S. (Edin.), F.C.S. Crown 8vo, cloth, Illustrated. 7s. 6d.
Pharmaceutical Journal.—"The subject is treated more thoroughly and
completely than in any similar work published in this country."

MANUAL OF ASSAYING GOLD, SILVER, COPPER,
and Lead Ores. By WALTER LEE BROWN, B.Sc. Revised, Corrected,
and considerably Enlarged, with a chapter on the Assaying of Fuel, &c.
By A. B. GRIFFITHS, Ph.D., F.R.S. (Edin.), F.C.S. Crown 8vo, cloth,
Illustrated, 7s. 6d.
Colliery Guardian.—"A delightful and fascinating book."
Financial World.—"The most complete and practical manual on everything
which concerns assaying of all which have come before us."

GEODESY. By J. HOWARD GORE. Crown 8vo, cloth, Illustrated, 5s.
St. James's Gazette.—"The book may be safely recommended to those who
desire to acquire an accurate knowledge of Geodesy."
Science Gossip.—"It is the best we could recommend to all geodetic students.
It is full and clear, thoroughly accurate, and up to date in all matters of earth-
measurements."

THE PHYSICAL PROPERTIES OF GASES. By
ARTHUR L. KIMBALL, of the Johns Hopkins University. Crown 8vo,
cloth, Illustrated, 5s.
Chemical News.—"The man of culture who wishes for a general and accurate
acquaintance with the physical properties of gases, will find in Mr. Kimball's
work just what he requires."

HEAT AS A FORM OF ENERGY. By Professor R. H.
THURSTON, of Cornell University. Crown 8vo, cloth, Illustrated, 5s.
Manchester Examiner.—"Bears out the character of its predecessors for
careful and correct statement and deduction under the light of the most recent
discoveries."

The Great Educators.

A Series of Volumes by Eminent Writers, presenting in their entirety " A Biographical History of Education."

The Times.—" A Series of Monographs on ' The Great Educators ' should prove of service to all who concern themselves with the history, theory, and practice of education."

The Speaker.—" There is a promising sound about the title of Mr. Heinemann's new series, ' The Great Educators.' It should help to allay the hunger and thirst for knowledge and culture of the vast multitude of young men and maidens which our educational system turns out yearly, provided at least with an appetite for instruction."

Each subject will form a complete volume, crown 8vo, 5*s.*

Now ready.

ARISTOTLE, and the Ancient Educational Ideals. By THOMAS DAVIDSON, M.A., LL.D.

The Times.—" A very readable sketch of a very interesting subject."

LOYOLA, and the Educational System of the Jesuits. By Rev. THOMAS HUGHES, S.J.

Saturday Review.—" Full of valuable information. . . . . If a school-master would learn how the education of the young can be carried on so as to confer real dignity on those engaged in it, we recommend him to read Mr. Hughes' book."

ALCUIN, and the Rise of the Christian Schools. By Professor ANDREW F. WEST, Ph.D.

The Times.—" A valuable contribution, based upon original and independent study, to our knowledge of an obscure but important period in the history of European learning and education."

FROEBEL, and Education by Self-Activity. By H. COURT-HOPE BOWEN, M.A.

The Scotsman.—" After a brief sketch of Froebel's career, Mr. Bowen deals exhaustively with his system of education."

ABELARD, and the Origin and Early History of Universities. By JULES GABRIEL COMPAYRÉ, Professor in the Faculty of Toulouse.

The Manchester Courier.—" The account of the general spirit and influence of the early universities are subjects scarcely less interesting than Abelard's own career, and are all capably treated by the author, who has throughout dealt with an important subject in a brilliant and able manner."

HERBART AND THE HERBARTIANS. By Prof. DE GARMO.

The Saturday Review.—" Remarkably clear, and will certainly be of the greatest service to the English student of the history of education."

In preparation.

ROUSSEAU ; and, Education according to Nature. By PAUL H. HANUS.

HORACE MANN, and Public Education in the United States. By NICHOLAS MURRAY BUTLER, Ph.D.

THOMAS and MATTHEW ARNOLD, and their Influence on Education. By J. G. FITCH, LL.D., Her Majesty's Inspector of Schools.

PESTALOZZI: or, the Friend and Student of Children.

Fiction.

New Three Volume Novels.

IN HASTE AND AT LEISURE.

By Mrs. Lynn Linton, Author of "Joshua Davidson," &c.

New Two Volume Novels.

HER OWN FOLK.

(EN FAMILLE.)

By Hector Malot, Author of "No Relations." Translated by Lady Mary Loyd. Crown 8vo, cloth. 12s.

A DRAMA IN DUTCH.

By Z. Z. Crown 8vo, cloth. 12s.

New One Volume Novels.

BENEFITS FORGOT.

By Wolcott Balestier. A New Edition. Crown 8vo, cloth 6s.

A PASTORAL PLAYED OUT.

By M. L. Pendered. Crown 8vo, cloth. 6s.

CHIMÆRA.

By F. Mabel Robinson, Author of "Mr. Butler's Ward,' &c.

MISS GRACE OF ALL SOULS'.

By W. Tirebuck.

THE MASTER.

By I. Zangwill.

TRANSITION.

By the Author of "A Superfluous Woman."

LITTLE STORIES ABOUT WOMEN.

By George Fleming

Popular 6s. Novels.

THE EBB-TIDE. By Robert Louis Stevenson and Lloyd Osbourne. Crown 8vo, cloth, 6s.

THE MANXMAN. By Hall Caine. Crown 8vo, cloth, 6s.

THE BONDMAN. A New Saga. By Hall Caine. Twenty-fifth Thousand. Crown 8vo, cloth, 6s.

THE SCAPEGOAT. By Hall Caine. Author of "The Bondman," &c. Thousand. Crown 8vo, cloth, 6s.

ELDER CONKLIN; and other Stories. By Frank Harris. 8vo, cloth, 6s.

THE HEAVENLY TWINS. By Sarah Grand, Author of "Ideala," &c. Forty-sixth Thousand. Crown 8vo, cloth, 6s.

IDEALA. By Sarah Grand, Author of "The Heavenly Twins." Tenth Thousand. Crown 8vo, cloth, 6s.

OUR MANIFOLD NATURE. By Sarah Grand. With a Portrait of the Author. Crown 8vo, cloth, 6s.

THE STORY OF A MODERN WOMAN. By Ella Hepworth Dixon. Second Edition. Crown 8vo, cloth, 6s.

A SUPERFLUOUS WOMAN. A New Edition. In One Volume. Crown 8vo, 6s.

AT THE GATE OF SAMARIA. By W.J. Locke. Crown 8vo, cloth, 6s.

A DAUGHTER OF THIS WORLD. By F. Battershall. Crown 8vo, cloth, 6s.

A COMEDY OF MASKS. By Ernest Dowson and Arthur Moore. A New Edition in One Volume. Crown 8vo, cloth, 6s.

THE JUSTIFICATION OF ANDREW LEBRUN. By F. Barrett. Crown 8vo, 6s.

THE LAST SENTENCE. By Maxwell Gray, Author of "The Silence of Dean Maitland," &c. Crown 8vo, cloth, 6s.

APPASSIONATA: A Musician's Story. By Elsa D'Esterre Keeling. Crown 8vo, cloth, 6s.

THE POTTER'S THUMB. By F. A. Steel, Author of "From the Five Rivers," &c. A New Edition. Crown 8vo, cloth. 6s.

FROM THE FIVE RIVERS. By Flora Annie Steel, Author of "Miss Stuart's Legacy." Crown 8vo, cloth, 6s.

RELICS. Fragments of a Life. By Frances Macnab. Crown 8vo, cloth, 6s.

THE TOWER OF TADDEO. By Ouida, Author of "Two Little Wooden Shoes," &c. New Edition. Crown 8vo, cloth. Illustrated. 6s.

CHILDREN OF THE GHETTO. By I. ZANGWILL,
Author of "The Old Maids' Club," &c. New Edition, with Glossary.
Crown 8vo, cloth, 6s.

THE PREMIER AND THE PAINTER. A Fantastic
Romance. By I. ZANGWILL and LOUIS COWEN. Third Edition. Crown
8vo, cloth, 6s.

**THE KING OF SCHNORRERS, GROTESQUES AND
FANTASIES.** By I. ZANGWILL. With over Ninety Illustrations. Crown
8vo, cloth, 6s.

THE RECIPE FOR DIAMONDS. By C. J. CUTCLIFFE
HYNE. Crown 8vo, cloth, 6s.

A VICTIM OF GOOD LUCK. By W. E. NORRIS, Author
of "Matrimony," &c. Crown 8vo, cloth. 6s.

THE COUNTESS RADNA. By W. E. NORRIS, Author of
"Matrimony," &c. Crown 8vo, cloth, 6s.

THE NAULAHKA. A Tale of West and East. By RUDYARD
KIPLING and WOLCOTT BALESTIER. Second Edition. Crown 8vo,
cloth, 6s.

AVENGED ON SOCIETY. By H. F. WOOD, Author of
"The Englishman of the Rue Cain," "The Passenger from Scotland
Yard." Crown 8vo, cloth, 6s.

THE O'CONNORS OF BALLINAHINCH. By Mrs.
HUNGERFORD, Author of "Molly Bawn," &c. Crown 8vo, cloth, 6s.

PASSION THE PLAYTHING. A Novel. By R. MURRAY
GILCHRIST. Crown 8vo, cloth, 6s.

Five Shilling Volumes.

THE SECRET OF NARCISSE. By EDMUND GOSSE.
Crown 8vo, buckram, 5s.

INCONSEQUENT LIVES. A Village Chronicle. By J. H.
PEARCE, Author of "Esther Pentreath," &c. Crown 8vo, cloth, 5s.

VANITAS. By VERNON LEE, Author of "Hauntings," &c.
Crown 8vo, cloth, 5s.

Two Shillings and Sixpence.

THE DOMINANT SEVENTH: A Musical Story. By
KATE ELIZABETH CLARKE. Crown 8vo, cloth, 2s. 6d.

The Pioneer Series.

12mo, cloth, 3s. net; or, paper covers, 2s. 6d. net.

The Athenæum.—"If this series keeps up to the present high level of interest, novel readers will have fresh cause for gratitude to Mr. Heinemann."
The Daily Telegraph.—"Mr. Heinemann's genial nursery of up-to-date romance."
The Observer.—"The smart Pioneer Series."
The Manchester Courier.—"The Pioneer Series promises to be as original as many other of Mr. Heinemann's ventures."

JOANNA TRAILL, SPINSTER. By ANNIE E. HOLDS-WORTH.

The Observer.—"Every word tells that it is the work of a true woman, who has thought deeply and lovingly on a most painful subject. . . . The picture is a beautiful one, which it would be well for many women to ponder over. In her claim for wider sympathy, a higher understanding of right and wrong, and her noble picture of woman helping woman, the authoress has done a good work."

GEORGE MANDEVILLE'S HUSBAND. By C. E. RAIMOND,

The Spectator.—"This very clever and terse story. . . . Mr. Raimond is undoubtedly an artist of great power. He certainly understands women's distinctive graciousness and ungraciousness as few women of the advanced type appear to understand it."
The Pall Mall.—"Clever, biting, and irresistible."

THE WINGS OF ICARUS. By LAURENCE ALMA TADEMA.

The Daily Telegraph.—"An intensely pathetic tale of passionate love and ineffable self-sacrifice. . . . Nothing has been more impressively told in the pages of modern fiction than the *dénouement* of this sad but deeply fascinating story."

THE GREEN CARNATION. By R. S. HICHENS.

The World.—"'The Green Carnation' is brimful of good things, and exceedingly clever. It is much more original, really, than its title implies. The character sketches are admirable and are probably drawn from the life."
The Observer.—"The book is a classic of its kind."

AN ALTAR OF EARTH. By THYMOL MONK.

The Speaker.—"It is not merely clever, but pathetic and natural."

A STREET IN SUBURBIA. By E. W. PUGH.

THE NEW MOON. By C. E. RAIMOND.

Other Volumes to follow.

UNIFORM EDITION OF

THE NOVELS OF BJÖRNSTJERNE BJÖRNSON.

Edited by EDMUND GOSSE.

Fcap. 8vo, cloth, 3s. *net* each volume.

Vol. I.—SYNNOVÉ SOLBAKKEN.

With Introductory Essay by EDMUND GOSSE, and a Portrait of the Author.

Vol. II.—ARNE.

To be followed by

A HAPPY BOY.	MAGNHILD.
THE FISHER MAIDEN.	CAPTAIN MANSANA.
THE BRIDAL MARCH.	AND OTHER STORIES.

UNIFORM EDITION OF

THE NOVELS OF IVAN TURGENEV.

Translated by CONSTANCE GARNETT.

Fcap. 8vo, cloth, price 3s. net, each volume.

Vol. I.—RUDIN.

With a Portrait of the Author and an Introduction by STEPNIAK.

Vol. II.—A HOUSE OF GENTLEFOLK.

Vol. III.—ON THE EVE.

To be followed by

Vol. IV.   FATHERS AND CHILDREN.

  ,,   V.   SMOKE.

  ,,   VI., VII.   VIRGIN SOIL.   (Two Volumes.)

Ibeinemann's International Library.

EDITED BY EDMUND GOSSE.

New Review.—" If you have any pernicious remnants of literary chauvinism I hope it will not survive the series of foreign classics of which Mr. William Heinemann, aided by Mr. Edmund Gosse, is publishing translations to the great contentment of all lovers of literature."

Each Volume has an Introduction specially written by the Editor
Price, in paper covers, 2s. 6d. each, or cloth, 3s. 6d.

IN GOD'S WAY. From the Norwegian of BJÖRNSTJERNE BJÖRNSON.

PIERRE AND JEAN. From the French of GUY DE MAUPASSANT.

THE CHIEF JUSTICE. From the German of KARL EMIL FRANZOS, Author of "For the Right," &c.

WORK WHILE YE HAVE THE LIGHT. From the Russian of Count LEO TOLSTOY.

FANTASY. From the Italian of MATILDE SERAO.

FROTH. From the Spanish of Don ARMANDO PALACIOVALDÉS.

FOOTSTEPS OF FATE. From the Dutch of LOUIS COUPERUS.

PEPITA JIMÉNEZ. From the Spanish of JUAN VALERA.

THE COMMODORE'S DAUGHTERS. From the Norwegian of JONAS LIE.

THE HERITAGE OF THE KURTS. From the Norwegian of BJÖRNSTJERNE BJÖRNSON.

LOU. From the German of BARON ALEXANDER VON ROBERTS.

DOÑA LUZ. From the Spanish of JUAN VALERA.

THE JEW. From the Polish of JOSEPH IGNATIUS KRASZEWSKI.

UNDER THE YOKE. From the Bulgarian of IVAN VAZOFF.

FAREWELL LOVE! From the Italian of MATILDE SERAO.

THE GRANDEE. From the Spanish of Don ARMANDO PALACIO-VALDÉS.

A COMMON STORY. From the Russian of GONTCHAROFF.

In preparation.
NIOBE. From the Norwegian of JONAS LIE.

Popular 3s. 6d. Novels.

CAPT'N DAVY'S HONEYMOON, The Blind Mother,
and The Last Confession. By HALL CAINE, Author of "The Bondman,"
"The Scapegoat," &c. Sixth Thousand.

A MARKED MAN: Some Episodes in his Life. By ADA
CAMBRIDGE, Author of "A Little Minx," "The Three Miss Kings,"
"Not All in Vain," &c.

THE THREE MISS KINGS. By ADA CAMBRIDGE.

A LITTLE MINX. By ADA CAMBRIDGE.

NOT ALL IN VAIN. By ADA CAMBRIDGE.

A KNIGHT OF THE WHITE FEATHER. By TASMA,
Author of "The Penance of Portia James," "Uncle Piper of Piper's
Hill," &c.

UNCLE PIPER OF PIPER'S HILL. By TASMA.

THE PENANCE OF PORTIA JAMES. By TASMA.

THE COPPERHEAD; and other Stories of the North
during the American War. By HAROLD FREDERIC, Author of "The
Return of the O'Mahony," "In the Valley," &c.

THE RETURN OF THE O'MAHONY. By HAROLD
FREDERIC, Author of "In the Valley," &c. With Illustrations.

IN THE VALLEY. By HAROLD FREDERIC, Author of
"The Lawton Girl," "Seth's Brother's Wife," &c. With Illustrations.

THE SURRENDER OF MARGARET BELLARMINE.
By ADELINE SERGEANT, Author of "The Story of a Penitent Soul."

THE STORY OF A PENITENT SOUL. Being the
Private Papers of Mr. Stephen Dart, late Minister at Lynnbridge, in the
County of Lincoln. By ADELINE SERGEANT, Author of "No Saint," &c.

NOR WIFE, NOR MAID. By Mrs. HUNGERFORD, Author
of "Molly Bawn," &c.

THE HOYDEN. By Mrs. HUNGERFORD.

MAMMON. A Novel. By Mrs. ALEXANDER, Author of "The
Wooing O't," &c.

DAUGHTERS OF MEN. By HANNAH LYNCH, Author of
"The Prince of the Glades," &c.

A ROMANCE OF THE CAPE FRONTIER. By BERTRAM
MITFORD, Author of "Through the Zulu Country," &c.

'TWEEN SNOW AND FIRE. A Tale of the Kafir War of
1877. By BERTRAM MITFORD.

ORIOLE'S DAUGHTER. By JESSIE FOTHERGILL, Author
of "The First Violin," &c.

THE MASTER OF THE MAGICIANS. By ELIZABETH
STUART PHELPS and HERBERT D. WARD.

THE HEAD OF THE FIRM. By Mrs. RIDDELL, Author
of " George Geith," " Maxwell Drewett," &c.

A CONSPIRACY OF SILENCE. By G. COLMORE,
Author of "A Daughter of Music," &c.

A DAUGHTER OF MUSIC. By G. COLMORE, Author of
"A Conspiracy of Silence."

ACCORDING TO ST. JOHN. By AMÉLIE RIVES, Author
of " The Quick or the Dead."

KITTY'S FATHER. By FRANK BARRETT, Author of
"The Admirable Lady Biddy Fane," &c.

MR. BAILEY-MARTIN. By PERCY WHITE.

A QUESTION OF TASTE. By MAARTEN MAARTENS,
Author of "An Old Maid's Love," &c.

COME LIVE WITH ME AND BE MY LOVE. By
ROBERT BUCHANAN, Author of " The Moment After," "The Coming
Terror," &c.

DONALD MARCY. By ELIZABETH STUART PHELPS,
. Author of " The Gates Ajar," &c.

IN THE DWELLINGS OF SILENCE. A Romance
of Russia. By WALKER KENNEDY.

LOS CERRITOS. A Romance of the Modern Time. By
GERTRUDE FRANKLIN ATHERTON, Author of " Hermia Suydam," and
" What Dreams may Come."

Short Stories in One Volume.

Three Shillings and Sixpence each.

EPISODES. By G. S. STREET, Author of "The Autobiography of a Boy."

WRECKAGE, and other Stories. By HUBERT CRACKAN-THORPE. Second Edition.

MADEMOISELLE MISS, and other Stories. By HENRY HARLAND, Author of "Mea Culpa," &c.

THE ATTACK ON THE MILL, and other Sketches of War. By EMILE ZOLA. With an Essay on the short stories of M. Zola by Edmund Gosse.

THE AVERAGE WOMAN. By WOLCOTT BALESTIER. With an Introduction by HENRY JAMES.

BLESSED ARE THE POOR. By FRANÇOIS COPPÉE. With an Introduction by T. P. O'CONNOR.

PERCHANCE TO DREAM, and other Stories. By MARGARET S. BRISCOE.

WRECKERS AND METHODISTS. Cornish Stories. By H. D. LOWRY.

Popular Shilling Books.

PRETTY MISS SMITH. By FLORENCE WARDEN, Author of "The House on the Marsh," "A Witch of the Hills," &c.

MADAME VALERIE. By F. C. PHILIPS, Author of "As in a Looking-Glass," &c.

THE MOMENT AFTER: A Tale of the Unseen. By ROBERT BUCHANAN.

CLUES; or, Leaves from a Chief Constable's Note-Book. By WILLIAM HENDERSON, Chief Constable of Edinburgh.

THE NORTH AMERICAN REVIEW.

Edited by LLOYD BRYCE.

Published monthly.   Price 2s. 6d.

THE NEW REVIEW.

NEW SERIES.

Edited by W. E. HENLEY.

Published Monthly, price 1s.

LONDON:

WILLIAM HEINEMANN,

21 BEDFORD STREET, W.C.

www.ingramcontent.com/pod-product-compliance
Lightning Source LLC
Chambersburg PA
CBHW020851020726
47497CB00005B/1358